ENCHANTMENTS AND ESCAPE ROOMS

A Spooky Games Club Mystery Book 2

AMY MCNULTY

Crimson Fox
PUBLISHING

 Created with Vellum

Chapter One

"*I*t's looking real nice back there."

Cable Woodward, my next-door neighbor's adult nephew, may have been entirely human, but he definitely had some kind of supernatural gift for sneaking up on me from behind.

Jostling my canvas sunhat, I wiped the sweat off my brow with my forearm and turned around. The chill October air wasn't even the culprit responsible for the reddening of my cheeks. That was all my hard work. "Thanks!" I shouted up to him over the fence separating our yards. "Do you feel like lending me a hand?"

Since he was fairly tall, his whole head was visible over the faded pine fence. He smirked, the smile lighting up his dark eyes behind his circular wire-rim glasses. "Dahlia Poplar, is the do-gooder witch of Luna Lane asking someone else for assistance for once?"

"I am," I said, grinning. It was something new to me, but I'd been getting more used to it over the past month since Cable had moved to town, albeit temporarily. Not that he was the *cause* of my newfound attitude, per se, but his arrival had been the beginning of a wild series of events that had involved a cursed board game, rescuing the souls of several Luna Lane citizens stuck in limbo, and arresting a centuries-old vampire whom the whole town had thought to be one of us. At least that was over. In the weeks since, life in Luna Lane had gone back to being peaceful and humdrum.

Every day I performed a good deed, and every day I staved off another of the silver stone scales that grew up the length of my left forearm from wrist to shoulder. There were still so many potions in my mother's book I could try to attempt to break this curse once and for all, but lately, that sense of urgency that had plagued me for most of my thirty years had waned.

Right now, I wanted to transform my yard into more like what it had been when my mother had been alive. A decade had passed and I'd let it grow wild, vines and bushes and weeds and brambles overtaking the front yard and my mother's garden in the back.

It'd seemed more witchy, I'd told myself. But that wasn't the whole truth of it. It had hurt too much to take over Mom's role. The garden had been *her* thing. But now, I was thinking enough time had passed. That, and a biting comment about my house seeming like the perfect final resting place for a witch turned fully to stone had kind of made me less attached to the wild and crazy overgrowth.

Cable's feet shuffled through the grass. "What do you need?"

I pointed my trowel in one gloved hand at a pile of weeds beside me. "Bring that to the big pile over by the house. I'm going to magic it all away."

Cable didn't laugh, but I could sense his amusement as he bent over to scoop it up. "Why don't you just magic it all into tidiness to begin with? It would save you from streaking your forehead with dirt and bits of grass."

Out of instinct, I put my gloved hand to my forehead to cover up my embarrassment. He laughed out loud.

"I think you just made it worse." Leaning closer, he picked at some brambles in my fiery-orange hair. The scents of old books and a pine-like musk that had to be his aftershave tickled my nostrils and my heart picked up a beat.

I scuttled rearward on my backside, planting my jeans-covered rear end in the soil. "I decided I'm doing this by hand."

"Except for the burn-the-brush part?"

"Except for that," I said. "I'm just trying to feel what Mom might have felt—although she never let it get so out of control that she had much brush to dispose of to begin with."

Cable's friendly smile slipped and he held up two large, solid hands, not a callus to be found on either of them. "Got any extra work gloves?" He spoke with a slight, strange-to-pinpoint accent, full of bits and pieces he'd picked up on his travels around the world growing up.

I gave him a closer inspection. As usual, he had on a light-colored dress shirt and a pair of khakis. Dressed like a professor even when on sabbatical halfway across the world from his university in Scotland for a semester. Hardly gardening attire.

I waved both hands at him. "GNINEDRAG ROF SSERD."

With a yelp, he fell on his backside, a surge of magical energy spinning up from his toes to his head.

Covering my mouth with my dirty work gloves to stifle a laugh, I spit as the soil came into contact with my lips, then I laughed again.

He stared at me, then he looked at his work-glove-covered hands. His patent leather shoes had been swapped for sneakers, his khakis and dress shirt for overalls and a cotton long-sleeved shirt. On top of his head was a dark brown straw hat that did a great job of shading his peach complexion from the late afternoon sun. I didn't know where, exactly, the hat had come from—the rest could at least be explained by magic transmuting the material he wore to something else—but it certainly completed the scarecrow look.

"Can you do *anything*?" he asked with wonder.

Scoffing, I went back to crouching. "Hardly. Admittedly, that was something new." Humming, I picked up my garden shears and cut away at the tomato vines that had congealed with some weeds to form a giant web. Maybe my magic *was* evolving after all the experimentation I'd done to find a cure for my curse.

Years before I'd been born, a powerful witch named Eithne Allaway had lived on the outskirts of Luna Lane, somewhere deep in the woods. It was only last month I'd learned that she had once been part of this town, and the fact that she'd claimed to have once been friends with my mother—the witch whose child she'd cursed before birth, the witch she herself had killed twenty years after my mother had arrived here.

All Mom would tell me was that Eithne had taken offense at Mom's natural inclination to help those around her—to use her witchy gifts when necessary but to roll up her sleeves and do the work like a normie human whenever possible, too.

So she'd cursed me to have to perform one good deed per day. On days when I didn't, I grew a stone scale. One day, if I stopped the good deeds, I would turn entirely to stone.

Mom had kept the scales small when she'd been alive, but as of late, they'd grown larger and larger. Ripping some weeds until they yanked from the soil roots and all, I stumbled backward. I ran a hand absentmindedly over the arm where my latest scale had grown. It was covered by a long-sleeved cotton shirt, but I knew it was the diameter of a baseball.

"Are you all right?" asked Cable, his arms stuffed with as much brush as he could handle.

I giggled. He looked more like a scarecrow than ever, the bits of scraggly vines and weeds hanging out from his grasp every which way.

"I'm fine," I said, straightening myself up onto my knees and clutching at the next clump of overgrowth that had to go.

"Does your arm hurt?" He lowered his voice. "Did you grow a new scale?"

"No." I shook my head. "I've been diligent. I finished my good deed this morning and decided to spend the rest of the day helping out myself."

Cable nodded. "Good. Remember, if you're ever cutting it close, just run over to our place. Uncle Milton and I can always have you do something quick."

"Thank you," I said. "But I'm not being careless anymore."

He didn't say anything for a moment, so I peeked at him out of the corner of my eye. His eyebrow was arched.

"Honest!" I swore. "I'm trying not to worry so much. I got so focused on ending the curse, I didn't put my whole heart into seeing the positive in it." Humming again, I brought an especially aromatic little white-petaled weed up to my nose.

"Huh," said Cable. "Well, I suppose you're right. Nothing wrong with helping others every day. Or in taking a break."

"Is that what you call this?" I tossed the weed flower beside me. "Taking a break?"

"I spent all morning on my research while Uncle Milton watched his soaps. So I'd say so. Time to get some sun, see another human face…" If I wasn't mistaken, his cheeks darkened somewhat as he stared at me under the shade of his wide-brim hat. He shuffled off, dragging the pile along with him to the clearing I'd indicated earlier.

Just as he reached the pile I'd started, Broomie popped up from the discarded brush, scaring Cable-the-scarecrow so much, he let out a deep, resounding scream and stumbled backward, flinging the weeds and brambles every which way.

Her brush shaking in a bristles-rubbing-together sound I'd come to infer was her way of laughing, Broomhilde, my enchanted broomstick, spun up into the air and caught as much of the scattered debris as she could before it fell to the ground. Then she tossed it nicely in the pile.

She'd been tasked with dragging it to the pile earlier, but she'd clearly gotten distracted. It was all right. I was used to it.

I was also used to her hiding and jumping out at Cable whenever he stopped by. She seemed to find it amusing that he'd found her so frightening the one time he'd visited as a kid. It had given her something of a big head, to tell the truth, to know that she had that kind of effect on someone.

Cable clutched a work glove to his overalls.

"She is never going to get bored of that, is she?" he asked dryly.

Broomie kept up her little bristly chuckling.

"Broomhilde," I called over to her. She snapped to and soared my way. I pet her brush with a work glove. "You know it's not nice to play tricks on people." Even if Eithne claimed it was a witch's true nature.

Cowed, Broomie sulked toward the back of the garden. Treacherously close to where—

"It doesn't bother you that a couple of bodies were buried in this garden?" Cable put his hands on his hips and watched Broomie. Her bristles dragged across the soil. I'd used magic to even it out before I'd decided to tackle the garden by hand. But there was no erasing the knowledge of what had been there—I didn't have Eithne's skills to manipulate memory.

"They're at rest," I said, referring to the Davises, who'd lived here long before I had. "That's enough for me."

Cable nodded and I reached for another vine, attempting to entangle it gently from some overgrown grass.

"Uh, Dahlia?" said Cable from behind me.

"Hmm?" I asked, yanking on an especially stubborn clump. My muscles strained with the effort, but I leaned forward, putting my whole back into it.

"Why is this hat stuck to my head?"

With a grunt, I managed to pull the whole weed out at once, tumbling backward. The dangling, dirt-caked roots shed onto my shirt as I glanced upside down to see what he was talking about.

With both gloved hands, he was gripping the brim of the straw hat I'd conjured up for him, and he tugged up on it—*hard*. It shifted slightly, but it may as well have been glued on his head.

"Oh!" I tossed aside the weed and scrambled to my feet.

Cable blanched and tugged again.

"Wait!" I cried out, trying to push down where he was pulling up. My gloves covered his, our fore-arms brushing. As I pulled away with a start, I real-ized his gloves weren't moving, either.

He pulled back, jumping, and started yanking on one glove. It didn't move.

"Stop!" I cried out, putting a hand gently on his.

"What's happening?" he asked, his voice a whisper.

I took a deep breath and winced. "I've never conjured clothes on someone out of thin air before."

"And?" he asked. "Does that mean you don't know what's wrong with me?"

"Well, I…" My heart thudded at the sight of his ashen face. "Now, don't panic. I have a theory."

"A *theory*."

"And a solution! *Probably*." I added that last word quieter.

His legs went wobbly and I dove in to support him. At five-nine, I could support most of him, though he still towered over me by a head.

"Do you want the solution first or the theory?" I asked.

"The solution!" he said, his voice quavering just a bit. For all the bulk and muscle on the guy, he sure had a sensitive demeanor. I supposed it suited his American literature professor persona.

I straightened him up, steadying him, then released him. "ESAELER TNEMTNAHCNE!"

His clothes shimmered as if obscured by a reflective light, but though some thread at the bottom of his overall hems grew loose, the whole enchantment seemed to crash with an almost audible thud.

"Dahlia…?" Cable licked his lips and looked upward, as if saying a prayer.

"It's okay," I said, my heart thudding. It wasn't really okay. But a thought struck me. "Broomie! My hat!"

Broomhilde snapped to it, gliding over the half-groomed garden and inside the open window over the kitchen sink. Within moments, she was back, my large, black witch's hat with a purple band on her shaft.

"Thank you," I said, swapping my sunhat for

my witch's cap. Its brim was so wide, it offered better protection, but I didn't want to dirty it. It'd already been smudged with para-paranormal last month, a corrupted double-dark-magic substance that could take more and more of my powers away the longer I spent near it and the more of it was nearby.

"That will help?" Cable asked hopefully.

"My hat harnesses magical energy," I said. "I can do magic without it, but not the complicated stuff."

Cable gestured at himself. "Looks like you managed this pretty well to me."

"Yeah, well…" I winced. "I wasn't really thinking. I couldn't conjure you up clothes out of nothing, so I think my magic turned the clothes you were wearing into the outfit I wanted for you."

His eyes widened. "I wasn't wearing a hat. Or gloves."

I shrugged one shoulder pitiably. "My theory is the magic made that out of your hair and… skin?"

Cable stumbled again, gripping on to a trellis for support.

"No, it's okay! I promise!" It better be. "ESAELER TNEMTNAHCNE!" I cried out again, both hands extended toward him.

With a breeze-like force, my magic traveled from my hands and to his body, his clothes unraveling, his hat revealing his mess of dark, wavy hair, his gloves fading to reveal his smooth, thick hands, his gardening outfit changing back to his professor casual attire.

I let out a sigh of relief.

Cable stood, his hands shaking as he gazed down on them. He looked up to me, then to his hands, then back.

"I'm sorry." I clasped my hands together in front of me and grimaced.

"Maybe let me know next time you're trying a new spell on me? I might have to sign a release first."

I laughed nervously. He probably wasn't kidding.

Chapter Two

*A*s I headed across the street for groceries the next morning, the door to Milton's house opened and out stepped Cable, a couple of reusable totes hiked up his arm.

Taking a deep breath, I paused and let him catch up to me. We stood on the sidewalk awkwardly, me clutching Broomhilde with both hands.

"So," I said.

"Good morning," he replied, a faint, forced smile on his lips.

Broomie wagged her brush head at him in innocent greeting and he flinched but seemed to be struggling not to give her the satisfaction of making him back down. She bristle-giggled at his reaction anyway.

"I really am sorry!" I blurted out again. It had

made for an awkward evening. I'd wrapped up the gardening for the day, he'd gone home looking about to be sick, and I'd spent the evening scouring Mom's potions book for a better stock of recipes to try—not just to break my curse, but to be a better witch in general.

Changing hair and flesh into clothing? That was something a wicked witch would do. I needed to be more careful, more vigilant when it came to casting enchantments.

The potions book offered so many options, but I just wished it were more straightforward. There were the tried and true power-boosting potions I relied on, but nothing ever had the title, "Potion to cure a curse" or "Potion to make you taller." It was always more vague than that. When they failed, I had no idea if it was because it was the wrong potion or because I'd brewed it wrong. With titles like "For lightening the load" or "For clarity," who could tell what they could actually do?

All out of answers, I'd spent a lot of the night staring at the Poplar family crest illustrated in the inside cover of the book. Or at least that was what my mom had told me it was when I'd asked as a child.

For some reason, that crest had been especially prominent in my mind last night as I'd flipped from one page to the next. I'd almost forgotten about it until recently, the illustration just part of the book's design. But last night, I'd always come back between looking up potions to stare at it, as if I were waiting for it to come to life and give me answers. Golden, shiny ink in the shape of a square, with small, pointed black designs in the corners. At the center was a red circle, a little oblong in shape. Around the circle, in the smallest possible letters:

Sit tibi terra levis.

Latin, no doubt. I'd never bothered to look it up before.

Reaching into the pouch on the belt at my hip, I pulled out my list of groceries as well as tincture ingredients I could use in the next batch of potions I'd whip up. All I'd need to do after that was head to the woods surrounding Luna Lane to pick up the rest. At the top of the list I'd scrawled that Poplar family motto, more because it had stuck in my head than due to any particular hope of discovering what it meant when I was out and about. I'd head to the library maybe and search the Internet when I had the chance. One of these days, I'd invest in a smart-phone or laptop and Wi-Fi myself. I'd avoided it so far because learning more about the outside world just made me sadder when I thought about how at this rate, I'd never actually see any of it.

Cable scratched the back of his head, wincing. "I'm really sorry I panicked like that."

"Are you kidding me? I was panicked, too."

"You didn't seem worried." He chuckled. "If I'd

known *you* were as panicked as I was, I think I might have fainted."

"Might have made the job of fixing you easier," I said. "Working on an unconscious subject."

His skin went paler.

"I'm kidding!" I said. Broomie decided to go for a little solo flight above our heads, trilling as if humming all the while. As she slipped out from my grip, I twirled a bit of my long, red hair around a finger. "I'm really bad at this apology thing. There's no excuse for what I did."

"You weren't *trying* to harm me."

"That doesn't matter," I said softly.

He nudged me gently on the arm. I had on my usual short-sleeved black dress today. I could feel the pressure through the stone scale he touched, but not the feel of his skin on mine. "It matters to me."

"It's better than doing something with bad intent," I agreed. "But it doesn't excuse it if the result is the same." I sighed. Cable just let me stand there awkwardly. "My mom could do anything," I said. "Well, almost anything."

She could minimize the effect of my curse by making the scales that grew rather small while she'd been alive. But she couldn't break the curse entirely. She couldn't cure elderly Mrs. Flores of her dementia before they'd both died, so I wouldn't have dared to try to cure Milton of his. Some things were just too delicate to tinker around with.

"Your mom had more practice," said Cable

generously. "And I'm willing to be a guinea pig—so long as I know that's what I'm signing up for." His Adam's apple bobbed nervously.

I smirked. I was starting to understand why Broomie enjoyed teasing him so much. "I won't experiment on you again. I promise."

He visibly relaxed, his shoulders rolling forward. His lips pursed as he got a look at the list in my hand. "Latin?"

"Huh? Oh." The motto. I handed him the list. "Did you study Latin in your preparation to teach American literature?"

"Yes and no," he said, adjusting his glasses as he read the words. "Not for my career, but just for fun." Of course he would find studying dead languages fun. He was brilliant, a cultured world traveler. "I wouldn't say I'm fluent, but I know this idiom. *Sit tibi terra levis, sit tibi terra levis*... Ah! It's often on gravestones."

Well, *that* didn't sound promising. "Gravestones?"

He handed the list back and adjusted his glasses. "I think it means, '*May the earth rest lightly on you*.' It's a very beautiful funerary blessing, I'd say."

"Yeah..." I tucked the list back into my pouch, almost like I wanted to hide the ominous motto away. But it was in my mom's potions book. I doubted I could hide such a thing. Cable had said it was a thing of beauty, but as a family motto, I felt like it portended something grim and dreary.

Even ominous.

"Where did you read that message?" Cable asked.

"Oh, uh… just in my potions book." I didn't explain that it was associated with the Poplar family crest.

"Hmm," said Cable, but before he could say more, the door to his uncle's house opened again and out stepped Doc Day, a woman in her sixties who, as usual, wore her white lab coat and her white hair in a bun. Stopping by Milton's in the mornings was among her routine.

"Good morning, Dahlia!" she said as she reached the end of the walk up to the house.

"Morning, Doc," I said, offering her a smile. She looked much better now that a vampire wasn't draining her of too much blood. More fresh-faced.

"Cable, your uncle is resting," she said. "He seemed especially lucid this morning," she added, clearly pleased.

"He did," Cable said. "Thank you for stopping by."

"Oh, Milton's always my favorite patient." Doc Day's light blue eyes sparkled. "Most days he's my *only* patient, but that's how I like things around here."

Doc Day was the only doctor for a town of three hundred, and as the town's resident witch, I could perform a few healing enchantments myself. Maybe not perfectly, if Grady Vadas's scarred arm was anything to go by. But better than what medicine could achieve alone in a pinch. "You two have a nice day," she called, heading down the walk toward downtown. "No getting into mischief. You too, Broomhilde."

Broomie angled upward, bending and shaking her handle like an arm as if to wave goodbye, but the trilling laughter she seemed to be trying to keep quiet came out in a rhythm astonishingly like "heh heh heh." Cable and I both chuckled nervously. I'd take a break from the garden for today—and keep an eye on this naughty broomstick when our neighbor was around.

"So, what are your plans for today?" asked Cable as we looked both ways and crossed the street that almost no car ever traveled down. Broomie stretched and soared overhead.

"Shopping," I said, nodding toward Vogel's general store. Milton's family used to run it, but he'd sold it to the Mahajans more than twenty years ago. "Then off to the woods. You?"

"The woods, huh?" Cable studied me curiously, but I wouldn't elaborate. "Shopping," he said in echo of me as he gestured to his tote bags. "Faine said she'd drop by with lunch, but before then, I wanted to grab everything for dinner."

"Don't you usually order dinner from Faine, too?" I asked.

We stopped in front of the store. "Well, yeah,

but it's fun to cook once in a while, too. Besides, it's Saturday."

Saturday? Oh, Saturday*!* "Games Club?" I asked, wincing. That was the night we'd decided on meeting up regularly. I couldn't believe I'd forgotten.

"Of course!" Cable smiled. "I can't believe you're never excited."

I'd thought he'd been kidding when he'd mentioned Luna Lane's Spooky Games Club—or so it was unofficially known by those who played in it—was still meeting up after we'd cracked the mystery behind the cursed board game. But he, Faine, and Virginia were too attached to the idea. We'd met every Saturday since, Milton joining us most of the time since the meetings took place at his house. And then a couple of times, Qarinah the vampire and her lover, normie Sherriff Roan, the man most like the dad I'd never known, had shown. Last week, Mayor Abdel, our immortal mummy mayor, and Chione, his normie great-great-great-etcetera granddaughter, had joined again, too. Even Goldie—normie general store co-owner—had gotten in on the affair. This week, if the club kept on growing, I'd bet half the town would show.

Everyone except the vampire Draven, though he'd been in the club longer than any of us—as long as Milton.

Draven and I still hadn't spoken since he'd revealed he'd purchased the cursed game as a lark from Eithne all those decades ago. That he'd *known*

Eithne had been in Luna Lane long before I'd been born to begin with. Come to think of it, I still didn't know what price he'd been willing to pay for Eithne's little gift to the Games Club in those early days. I didn't know what price Ravana had paid for Eithne's darker magic in helping the vampire cover up the deaths and blood madness that had resulted from her drinking too many of Luna Lane's citizens dry all those years back.

"We'll have three tables out," said Cable, as if reading my mind about the club growing too big and misjudging my concern. "Snakes and Ladders for Milton—he's keen on that one and less likely to cheat, so Virginia will be happy—and Othello and chess for any overflow."

"We might be getting too big," I said. Broomie hovered in front of the general store window and peered inside, twirling excitedly when Goldie noticed her and waved.

"At least with Evidence, we were all playing *together*—"

"You want to play the cursed game?" Cable asked with a laugh. "It's still up in our attic. Milton didn't want to part with it, despite all the bad memories. It was his wife's and friends' home for too long."

Soul prison was more like it. But it had probably saved their souls in the long run, so I couldn't be too pedantic about that.

"*No!*" I said quickly. Too quickly. I shrugged.

"It's just… A Games Club makes me think of, like, *group* activities, you know?" If I was going to get my nose out of my potions book and my mom's garden to hang out with so many of Luna Lane's citizens at once, I at least didn't want it to devolve into a game parlor where only small groups interacted with one another. It just seemed to defeat the purpose.

The door to Vogel's opened, the overhead bell jingling.

"Dahlia, Cable, Broomhilde, darlings." Goldie wore a teal sari today beneath her white Vogel's apron, her black-and-gray hair in a side-bun. "Don't just stand there on the sidewalk like a couple of loiterers. Come in, come in."

We followed her past a conspicuously empty display at the front that could be seen through the store window—something was getting prime retail space for the season. Broomie chirped and zoomed around Goldie, pausing just long enough for the older woman to laugh and pat her once, then zipping inside toward the produce and the bin of discarded cornhusks Broomie subsisted on.

"Broomhilde, you could say *hello* to me first," said Arjun, Goldie's husband. Dressed in his usual khakis and dress shirt—much like Cable, come to think of it—beneath his Vogel's apron, he had one hand out toward the stack of apples. His thinning, mostly white hair had a bit of corn silk dangling from it that Broomie must have kicked up in her ravenous dining.

Broomie stuck her brush head out from the bin and let out a little gurgling sound akin to a burp. Then she seemed to notice the errant corn silk and slurped it right up, tickling Arjun's head. The poor man shrieked.

Even Cable chuckled at that one.

"Sorry," I said, wincing. "When it comes to food, she knows no manners."

My companion broomstick repeatedly brushed up against Arjun in a feline manner, insisting he put his apples down and pet her in forgiveness. He did, murmuring sweetly to her all the while. She knew how to get her way.

"What do you need?" asked Goldie, sweeping in beside us and holding out a hand to both of us.

The Mahajans liked to stay busy—and that included doing the shopping for their customers. I took my list out of the pouch on the golden belt at my waist and passed it over, but not before muttering under my breath, "ESARE" to the ominous Latin blessing so no one would ask awkward questions. Almost as one with me, Cable whipped his list out of his shirt pocket, used to the routine here in Luna Lane already.

Goldie beamed and looked knowingly—*too* knowingly—from Cable to me and back again. "You know, I once wished for Dahlia to marry Zashil, my younger son."

Why in the world was she bringing this up now —in front of Cable? My cheeks reddened.

"Hitesh," Arjun corrected, taking another apple from the wooden crate beside him and putting it perfectly on the stack in front of him. Broomhilde perched on his shoulders, curling around his neck. "Our eldest son."

"We didn't always know Zashil would marry a man," said Goldie, scolding her husband as she snatched our lists from us.

"Maybe *you* didn't. But I did. And I thought brainy Dahlia would make a perfect match for our intelligent Hitesh."

"And I thought Dahlia's adventurous spirit would make a better match for Zashil," said Goldie, her tone brokering no argument.

Intelligent and adventurous. Me, the witch cursed to stay in one town forever, the brainiac who'd accidentally turned her friend's scalp into a hat. They clearly thought too highly of me.

"You flatter me," I said. "But we were always just friends. And besides… 'adventurous' is hardly what I'd call a witch unable to leave town."

Cable watched me—too closely—and I was reminded of when he'd tricked me into thinking he was some amateur journalist, about to uncover the town's secret.

Which he'd actually known all along.

Again, intelligence was not my strong suit, either.

"You can't leave town?" he asked.

I shrugged, though the heaviness in my heart

hardly warranted such a casual response. "Part of the curse."

"So I guess I can't invite you to visit Scotland with me someday?" His voice was soft, introspective.

He was going to invite me to Scotland?

I felt excited and sick all at once. It could never happen. Not unless I broke this curse.

So far, I was zero for countless times trying to.

Goldie grabbed a couple of shopping baskets and draped them expertly over both arms, quickly going to work up and down the aisles.

"Maybe you were right, dear. Hitesh. Javier is an angel as a son-in-law, but Indira is a daughter-in-law who takes far too much after her own mother."

"You were the one who introduced them," said Arjun. He smirked at us as he picked up the empty crate. Broomie was hooked on him tightly, not even concerned with the movement. "The daughter of her best friend from back home."

"Best *rival* is more like it," said Goldie from somewhere several aisles over. The store wasn't as large as grocery stores I'd seen on TV, but it was plenty large for the rather short Goldie to seemingly disappear behind rows of aisles.

"*All* her friends back home were rivals," said Arjun quietly.

"I heard that!" said Goldie loudly.

The laughter was infectious. Arjun tossed his empty crate atop a stack of similar ones. "Dahlia, have you performed your good deed for the day?" he asked.

"No," I admitted sheepishly. "But I was going to ask before I left. I hoped to knock one off quickly before I head to the woods for the rest of the day."

"The woods?" asked Goldie. "Does that have something to do with these ingredients you asked for? Peppermint oil? Ginger root? You're either making a delicious dessert or you're brewing something again. If it's the former, I would like to invite myself over before Games Club."

"You'll be the first to know next time I bake a cake," I said. "But I've got a few things I want to brew."

Goldie popped out around the corner of an aisle, both baskets already half-full. "You cannot be late for Club." She glanced at one of the baskets. "Especially if Cable here is making what I think he is."

"If she *is* late, I'll head on over there and bring her over myself," added Cable.

"Really?" I said. "You sure you want to risk it?"

Cable blanched just a little, but his lips quirked up in a half-smile. "Just give me a warning next time."

"Oh?" said Goldie, her cheeks rosy. "What do you mean?"

Cable spun on her. "Do you like haggis?" He must have been referring to the dish he had planned. It sounded... terrible.

"I do," said Goldie, beaming. She wagged a finger at the two of us, though, as if to say she'd let her suspicions go, but not forever. "I cannot wait to see how your recipe turns out."

"She just wants to compare it to her own so she can spend the evening telling you which spices you used too little of," said Arjun. His wife shushed him and went back to shopping. Arjun tapped a hand to my shoulder, stroking Broomie's brush over his shoulder with the other hand. "Dahlia, will you please help me? Take those crates to the backroom and bring out what's left from Jeremiah's delivery this morning. They need to be put on display." He gestured to the empty display space by the door.

He knew just how to phrase it. An invisible sense of purpose took me over. I quickly headed for the stash.

"I'll help," said Cable, but the three of us responded, "No!" as Cable's hand reached for the crate below mine.

"Right." Cable cleared his throat and stepped back. "Your good deed for the day. I'm sorry."

"Don't be," I said. "It's nice to have someone who keeps offering to lend me a hand."

"*Keeps?*" repeated Goldie, and I tried my best to hide my flushing cheeks behind the stack of crates I now cradled to my chest.

Weaving through the aisles, I kicked the swinging door to the backroom just as the general store's phone rang.

"Vogel's General Store," answered Arjun. "Zashil! We were just talking about you."

I didn't hear the rest as I made my way to the back, only Goldie's squealing as she said, "*Beta!*" and headed for the phone her husband held.

The backroom to Vogel's was clean and well-organized, not so much as a slip of paper out of place. I knew right where to put the crates. Today must have been a big shipment from Jeremiah's farm. He kept them topped off with fresh produce every day, but every once in a while, they'd have a productive harvest and send in a mass of stuff. With Halloween around the corner, it was only fitting that the boxes that remained contained squashes, gourds, and large pumpkins perfect for carving. Arjun's back wasn't what it used to be, so it made sense he'd ask for help.

"Okay," I said out loud, staring down the seven boxes in front of me. No magic, so I couldn't just zap them out front or levitate them in front of me. Time to exercise the old muscles.

"That's wonderful!" Goldie's voice was so loud, it carried out across the store all the way to me back here. "Yes, yes, of course!" I was sure she'd tell me all about whatever news Zashil had to share.

I bent down to grab the crate of pumpkins. Start with the heaviest first, make the rest go smoother.

With a grunt, I managed to get the thing about

an inch off the ground before a sharp cramp shot across my lower back.

"Come on," I said through gritted teeth. "Lift with the legs, not the back." Repositioning myself, I tried again with just as much success.

"Ouch, ouch, ouch," I said, putting the crate back down. I stared down at it. The top pumpkin seemed to be looking at me. It was fairly ripe, but it had grown dented and twisted, and I could already see where the eyes and mouth would go. They were practically sneering at me.

As long as it didn't directly accomplish my task, I could get away with *a little* bit of magic during my good deeds.

"NIAP ON," I said, gesturing my arms at my back. Something soft tickled over my skin, the enchantment taking effect.

"Still think you're so tough, mister?" I said to that pitted pumpkin. I bent down, lifting with my knees, and found no resistance from my back despite the slight strain on the muscles all over my body. "Ha." I laughed at that pitted pumpkin and made my way back to the storefront.

Goldie was still on the phone, her voice light and bubbly as she spoke in Hindi, swaying back and forth. Arjun was packing up Cable's purchases.

Cable's eyes bulged as I made my way to the produce. "Should you be carrying all that by yourself?"

Crouching, I set the crate down by the empty

display beside the door with a satisfying little thud. "I told you. I have to do these deeds alone."

"But that much at *once*?"

I stood, my back stiff. It didn't hurt, but there was definitely something off about it. I rubbed at it, the relaxing sensation traveling through my muscles and down to my bones.

"Oh, dear, Dahlia, please be careful," said Arjun, rushing to my side. Broomie perked up at the panic in his tone, sliding off his shoulders.

"I was very gentle with them," I protested, tickling Broomie under her brush. She seemed to relax, settling down by the cash register but flicking her handle off the front of the counter like a lazy cat's tail.

"I mean with yourself, dear!" Arjun frowned as he looked at my back. "I should have divvied that one up into two crates. Did you pull your back?"

"No, I…" I rubbed at it. "I don't think so." I *had* made it so I wouldn't feel pain in that spot, so actually, I couldn't be sure.

Arjun looked relieved. "Okay, then, but please be more careful." I knew he would have done this himself if I hadn't come along. And he had several decades on me. Surely, he was overreacting.

"I will, I will," I said. I headed back and got the next crate, following that up with two more. Cable left between boxes two and three, apologizing that he needed to check on his uncle and get the dinner started, and Goldie was still on the phone. Arjun finished ringing up my order by the time I put the last squash on display. It was a simple task, but it was enough. Like a held breath at last escaping my lips, the task was complete and my good deed was completed for the day, a tingling sensation on my arm where a new scale might have otherwise formed fading as the curse acknowledged the good deed.

I rubbed at my back as Goldie finally got off the phone and started jabbering away to Arjun faster than I could keep up with, half in English and half in Hindi. Broomie, having gone over to the door to inspect my work, poked her brush out from behind the pitted pumpkin I'd set at the top of the squash display by the door and I pet her absentmindedly.

I still really wanted to carve that bulbous gourd just so I could arrange that smirk pitted on its face.

"Oh, thank you," said Arjun, stepping over some minutes later. "Wonderful work, Dahlia. Wonderful!"

Goldie stepped up beside him and gripped his arm, practically bursting at the seams. "Did you tell her?"

"I just walked over here," said Arjun, shaking his head.

"Tell me what?" I asked as Broomie curled up in my arms.

"Zashil and Javier!" said Goldie, her voice almost song-like. "They're moving to Luna Lane and opening a business!"

"Zashil is," corrected Arjun. "With his new business partner. Javier's an artist who can work anywhere."

"Oh!" I said. "That's wonderful." And odd. I'd thought both Mahajan brothers had been only too happy to put Luna Lane and its oddities behind them. "Does Javier know…?" I asked, ever worried about the secret of Luna Lane escaping to the world.

"Of course!" said Goldie, playfully slapping me. "He's family. Both he and Indira have been shown when they visit for holidays."

"Yes, of course," I said. I'd been invited a few times for dinner when either brother and his family were in town, but I'd never shown up in full witch garb or enchanted the salt and pepper shakers my way. Another thought struck me. "But this 'business partner'?"

"Hmm." Arjun frowned.

"Who can say?" said Goldie, undeterred. "We'll have to meet him and decide. It doesn't sound like he plans to move to town, just get the business up and running and move on to another location. Apparently, he franchises all across the country."

"Franchises what?" I asked. "What kind of business does Zashil hope to bring to Luna Lane?"

"Hope to? It's a done deal!" said Goldie excitedly. "He bought the old bowling alley without a *word* to us—wanted to make sure he got all his investments sorted. Investments? Our son, attracting *investors*!" She was practically *choking* Arjun's arm.

"The bowling alley? Oh. Bowling in Luna Lane once more."

I had mixed feelings. Bowling might be fun, and there'd been one in our small town before. But that was also where I'd confronted Ravana last month, where her wicked plans had been revealed and poor Grady had lost an arm. Before I'd reattached it.

I wasn't sure I could send a bowling ball down those lanes without all of that history popping up in my brain. Even bowling balls were tainted now that I knew what my grandma figure, Leana, had done with one of them.

"Oh, no, I don't mean he'll *reopen* the bowling alley," said Goldie, her mouth still several seconds behind her brain, no doubt. "Zashil is opening an escape room! He assures me they're quite popular, even in small towns like Luna Lane."

An *escape room*? I'd never been out of town, so I'd never been to one. But I'd read about them, had seen them popping up here and there on TV.

They certainly were a fad to be reckoned with if they were coming as far as Luna Lane.

"Huh," I said. But would three hundred customers be enough? Or a fraction thereof, since I doubted everyone from Doc Day to Mayor Abdel and Jeremiah the farmer would want to play.

Did that mean he hoped to attract people from out-of-town?

My heart sunk. I needed to meet with Zashil as soon as he showed up. It sounded like the plan was already in motion, but had he really thought it through? What tourists could do to the peace and tranquility of Luna Lane?

"Why, Games Club should be the first to play!" said Goldie.

Arjun *tsked*. "I thought he promised his family the first game."

"The second, then." Goldie practically bounced on her feet. "My baby's coming home." She patted Broomie gently before turning on her heel, humming her way to the backroom.

I couldn't bring myself to rain on her parade.

And had she said *Games Club*?

Well, I *had* wished for something we could all do as a group, so long as everyone was insistent on keeping the thing going.

"Let me get your things packed," said Arjun. He seemed airier, too, lighter, like nothing could possibly ruin his day.

"Oh. Yeah." I scrambled in my pouch for my folded-up reusable tote, and this time, I produced more than enough money. I'd been better at remembering to zap the money out from the other dimension in which Mom had stored it every morning.

"You keep that," said Arjun, taking just my bag from me. "Payment for the help."

"Don't be silly," I said, following him back to the

register. When he wasn't looking, I slipped the bill into the "take a penny, leave a penny" tray.

He handed me my bag and Broomie flew up to curl around my shoulders, the tip of her handle hanging down like the tail of the nine cats she'd once been before choosing to live her last, extra life as a witch's broom.

"Do you need help carrying this home?" Arjun asked, passing over the bulging tote.

"No, I'm fine. Don't worry," I said, taking it from him. I slipped it over my arm and felt the muscles in my lower back stretch uncomfortably. "I'm so happy to hear about Zashil," I said genuinely. My misgivings would have to come later —and have to be told to him directly. Perhaps he could do something else with the building and still stay.

"You must dine with us," he said. "They're arriving tomorrow."

"That's fast," I said. "All right. Just let me know when and if I should bring anything."

"Just yourself," said Arjun, smiling. "Oh, but maybe Cable as well?"

"You'll have to ask him." I chuckled. These two would matchmake for me yet, apparently. I waved and started walking to the door, my back stretching oddly with each movement. Then I realized I ought to lift the enchantment, just to make sure I hadn't damaged anything.

It was definitely fine, but best to be sure.

"ESAELER TNEMTNAHCNE." I waved my hands behind my back.

And then I fell to the ground in excruciating pain.

It might have been my imagination, but I swore the last thing I saw as blackness caved in on the corners of my vision was that darn pitted pumpkin cackling down at me.

Chapter Three

"And then Milton was like, 'I'm climbing to the top of the board!' and I had to show him *three times* that his ladder didn't reach that high. It reached to the row *beneath* the top."

I blinked bleary eyes to come face to face with a ghost. My friend, but a ghost nonetheless.

Virginia Kincaid, resident Luna Lane specter with unfinished business, the specifics of which she'd never quite articulate with any of us. Personally, I figured she just liked hanging around at this point.

"And anyway, it was dreadfully dull with everyone so worried about you. We took turns watching over you all night. She's fine, I told them. Doc Day said she just passed out from the pain. You'd be right as rain as soon as you woke up and healed yourself."

Pain? Passed out? *All night*? I shifted up in bed, my back seizing with the slightest movement, and I cried out, falling back onto my mattress. I was in my bedroom somehow, the *tick, tick, tock* of Mom's cuckoo clock echoing in my head.

"Oh, Mrs. Mahajan left this for your breakfast. She and Mr. Mahajan felt so bad." Virginia gestured her pale, pale white lace-covered hand toward the bedside table. There was a covered porcelain bowl there, from which wafted the scent of coconut. "You missed the haggis Mr. Woodward made, but judging by the looks on everyone's faces, I'd have to say that's a *good* thing. I can't even smell anymore, and I could tell it reeked."

Her delicate features scrunched up in disgust.

She kept talking and I stared blankly at her, everything about her faded from head to toe. She was forever twenty-one, as she so often reminded us, decked out in turn-of-the-twentieth-century conservative attire, with a long, white skirt and a blouse that covered everything right up to the middle of her neck. It had puffy sleeves over the shoulders and ruffles along the front. Above delicate buttons sat a faded red gem brooch. Her straw-colored hair was tucked into a carefully crafted bun beneath a broad white hat. Hovering over a chair at my bedside, she was without the lacy parasol she sometimes conjured up to "protect" her fair skin from sunlight. The same parasol with a porcelain handle and ferrule that she'd used to save me from a vampire bite last month.

"Ginny," I said softly, cutting her off. "How long have I been out?"

She tapped her chin. "About twenty-four hours, I'd venture."

I groaned. There had been so much I'd had planned for yesterday. Exploring the woods, trying out potions and enchantments. Games Club, too. Trying Cable's cooking for the first time.

My stomach rumbled at the coconut scent.

Broomie's brush perked up as I shifted onto my side, letting out a moan with the movement. She'd been curled up at my feet.

My arms strained as I shimmied them behind my back, pointing my palms at it. "LAEH." I should have just done that to begin with every time my back had hurt, but I probably wouldn't have been able to lift the crate then regardless.

Of course, then I might have done the smart thing and carried its contents in fewer trips.

Like the muscles had all been in a knot and were now unwinding, the pain seeped out from my body and faded into nothingness. I let out a sigh of relief and patted Broomie as her bristles rustled against my cheek.

"I'm okay, I'm okay," I told her.

I reached for a glass of water on the table next to whatever Goldie had brought.

"That's what I said would happen." Virginia crossed one ankle over the other, resting both hands atop one knee. "You could heal such a minor injury, no problem. The only issue was you had to be awake for it, and none of us could do that for you."

Sighing, I sat up and frowned. I had no one to blame but myself, but I'd lost a day and now I had to get out there and do another good deed before I could consider searching the woods for more ingredients.

Truth be told, every time I'd gone to the woods in the past month, I'd searched for remnants of Eithne's cottage, too. But I hadn't found any. Surely, it had been destroyed or I'd have noticed it sooner.

I could ask Draven… But I hadn't spoken to him since that night. As if things with my vampire ex-boyfriend hadn't been awkward enough before I'd learned about the secrets he'd been keeping from me.

Mayor Abdel had said he'd known Eithne had been out there, but he'd never availed himself of her services, so he'd never seen her in person at all. I supposed I couldn't blame him for not mentioning the fact that she'd lived outside of town before my mom had moved here. It wasn't like we were particularly close, and I'd never asked him.

Draven, on the other hand… He'd known what I thought of the silver-haired witch.

"Miss Poplar?" Virginia asked. I must have been staring off into space. "Here." She held a hand out and with a little squint of her eyes, her color grew slightly more solid. She reached for the bowl Goldie had left behind and handed it to me, her efforts having turned at least part of herself corporeal. "Eat up. I can hear your stomach rumbling from here."

I smiled flatteringly at her and took the bowl gladly, as well as the spoon she handed me when she took the lid away. It was *Ven Pongal*. Goldie had made it for me before. A comfort food for her sons growing up.

It tasted like heaven on my tongue.

"You know, it was Mr. *Cable* Woodward who carried you home," said Virginia, her body leaning forward conspiratorially.

I almost dropped the spoon. It wouldn't have been the first time I'd been in his arms, but I wasn't *trying* to make a habit of it. And it'd have been nice to have been conscious for it.

I couldn't believe I'd just thought that.

"Mr. and Mrs. Mahajan just didn't know what to do. One called for Doc Day, while the other ran across the street to put those strapping arms to good use." Virginia smiled, but then she sighed, the sparkle in her eyes dimming somewhat. "I was betrothed, you know."

Instead of rolling my eyes at her telling me that for the five hundredth time since she'd first shown herself to me when I'd been around ten, I grabbed for her hand. It was still corporeal, though it felt icy cold beneath the lace. Still, I didn't flinch. She was a true friend; she'd proven that to me.

Virginia seemed a little taken aback, but her

shoulders soon relaxed. "I just… I just don't want you to lose out on an opportunity for love. Not with such a good match. And he's a *nice* man." Her voice cracked. The way she'd said it…

"Ginny, was your betrothed a nice man?"

She produced a handkerchief out of nowhere and dabbed at her eyes. I wasn't sure whether or not she could still actually cry.

"You know, you're nine years older than I was when I passed, *well beyond* spinster age."

"Thanks." I groaned. So much for trying to listen to what she had to say for once. "You know, women don't *have to* get married or be shunned these days."

"There was also joining the convent. There was a quite foreboding one in Creekdale, I used to think. The nuns used to narrow their eyes if you so much as glanced at them or bade them *hello*."

I chuckled. A witch joining a convent somewhere. I didn't think I would fit in. Or maybe I would in this one in Creekdale, judging by the harsh looks the nuns had given poor Virginia back in the day. Maybe it was all a front for a coven of witches. But I was never getting out of town at this rate, least of all to investigate a convent.

"I'm just saying." Virginia stood, though it was more like she hovered, some of her skirt even billowing through my bed. "You don't want to die with regrets like I did." Though she didn't really seem worse for wear because she'd hung around a hundred or so extra years. She produced her parasol and opened it, resting it upon one shoulder. Good thing she didn't believe in superstitions like not opening an umbrella indoors. "In any case, I promised to tell everyone as soon as you woke."

Putting Goldie's dish down, I flung off the covers. "No, wait, I can just—"

But off she went, floating through my door and leaving behind a trail of green ectoplasm to clean.

I looked down at my dress, at the sweat that dotted it. My hair clung to my forehead. "NAELC," I said, gesturing to myself, to my dress, to the doorway.

That was one enchantment at least I never messed up. I used it so frequently.

Falcon stared at me as I stood on the top of the café's stepstool, reaching the sponge up, up, up until I touched the top of the café's front window. The grime really got caked there the longer you went without cleaning it.

Though the pain was nothing compared to what I'd just experienced, the soreness in my shoulders and arms as I worked on the second half of the window dug in deep. But I wasn't going to cheat even a little today. Nope. I wouldn't make that mistake again. If I hurt something, I'd better know about it.

"Aren't you cold, honey?" I asked the three-year-old staring up at me.

He sucked on his thumb, his dark eyes wide. His puppy-design T-shirt was a little crooked, his pants a bit stained. He and his dad and sisters had just come back from the woods, spending their Sunday afternoon at play. How I wished I had a day off once in a while. Well, one that didn't end in me growing a new stone scale on my skin.

The door to Hungry Like a Pup popped open and the overhead bell rang. Flora, Faine and Grady's eldest at seven years old, stepped out. "Falcon, Mommy says you can't bother Auntie Dahlia right now."

The two siblings looked a lot alike—as did their other sister, five-year-old Fauna. Medium brown complexion, curly dark brown hair, their mom's freckles and their dad's eyes. Flora was more put together than her brother, though she'd missed a bramble that still stuck to the back of her hair.

"It's all right," I told her. "As long as he stays on the sidewalk where I can see him." I winked at him.

He giggled and walked over to the sudsy bucket below, reaching for another sponge.

"Oh, no, honey, thank you, but I can do it myself."

"I'm a big boy!" Falcon looked up at me, puzzled, the sponge in hand.

"I know you are, Falcon. And you're very nice to offer your help, but I have to do it alone." I climbed down the stepstool and bent down to wring out the sponge in the bucket. Even my thighs were aching.

Flora grabbed his hand and nudged him until he dropped the sponge. "You can only sometimes help Auntie Dahlia, remember?" she asked him. "She was cursed by a witch."

"She *is* a witch?" asked Falcon.

"Yes, I'm a witch." I winked again. "But I still need to help out just like the rest of you. Why don't you go inside and help your mom and dad? That would be a *big* help from a big boy!"

Pleased with my praise, he allowed his sister to drag him back, slapping those dirt-caked sneakers on the concrete like they weighed fifty pounds.

I swapped my sponge for the one Falcon had almost helped with and sighed. It somehow just cut a little deep to be teaching a toddler eager to help that he wasn't to help me at all. But at least he'd taken to the "cursed by a witch" explanation as if it made perfect sense.

He was a werewolf, after all. And ever since he'd gotten into the habit of wandering off by himself to offer his blood to a vampire, his family had kept a closer watch on him. He'd only just started feeling better, the vampire venom addiction fading from his system within the past few days.

Though he still managed to slip out from under their grasp, as evidenced by the fact that he'd been out here watching me.

Inside the café, Broomie buzzed around over

everyone's head, little pigtailed Fauna scrambling after her and trying to reach up to grab her handle. Faine just barely managed to avoid the two of them slamming into her as she carried two plates out to Mayor Abdel and Chione. Grady was at the register, Flora teaching Falcon to wipe the nearby counter down with a damp rag.

After a few more minutes of scrubbing, I slid back down the stepstool, satisfied.

Like a rush of relief through my system, the good deed for the day was complete. Grady and Faine had kept meaning to wash their café windows, but they'd never managed to find time.

Good thing for them I had to *make* the time for little tasks like that.

Tossing the sponge back into the bucket, I stepped back to admire my handiwork, planting my hands on my lower back and rolling my shoulders to get the kinks out.

"Still doing all the chores in town?"

The voice was deep—and familiar.

I turned around. Zashil stood just an inch or so shorter than me, his lean physique chiseled into more bulk than I remembered. His black, wavy hair had just the slightest strings of silver woven through-out, his straight nose so like his mom's and his puffy cheeks just like his dad's.

"Zashil!" I said, holding my arms out for a hug.

We hadn't had a chance to say another word before the bell over the door jingled again and out stepped Faine, crying out the name of our child-hood friend with even more relish than I had.

She swept him into a hug as well. "Your mother told us you were coming back! How exciting!" She glanced over his shoulder. "Where's Javier?"

"Back at Mom and Dad's," he said, slipping a hand into his jeans pocket. "Mom's keeping him plenty busy. I think they're cooking up enough food for the rest of the year."

Which reminded me, I needed to return her bowl. I'd knocked on Milton's door to thank Cable for his help, but Faine had been there instead to check in on Milton and deliver his lunch. She'd told me Cable had gone on some errands in the next town over, which I should have figured from the fact that his little tan smart car had been missing from the driveway. She'd offered to help me take care of my good deed for the day, and off I'd went with her. It had actually all worked out. Goldie would have made more of a fuss than even Virginia, and the next time I saw Cable would be awkward.

Best to just get on with my day.

"Virginia's there. She said you hurt yourself at Vogel's yesterday?" That was addressed to me.

"Oh, yeah, but I'm fine." My lips quirked into a smile. "So… How'd Javier take to Virginia?"

"He's met her before when we've been in town. He's a good listener, she's a good talker—it's a match made in heaven." He fluffed his hand at me. "It was actually Fred I was worried about…"

"Fred?" asked Faine.

"My business partner." Zashil looked over his shoulder, as if waiting for the man himself to show.

Right. I'd wanted to talk to him about that.

"But he'd gone ahead to scout the property before she showed up. He's supposed to meet me here any minute." He took his phone out of his pocket and checked the screen.

"I was hoping to talk to you——" I said at the same time Zashil himself said, "I was hoping I'd run into you." He locked eyes with me.

I cocked my head. "Does this have to do with keeping my magic out of Fred's sight? Believe me, you won't have to worry about that."

"No." Zashil cleared his throat and slipped his phone into his pocket. "When I said I was glad Fred wasn't there to see Virginia, I only meant because, well… it's one thing to hear someone talk about ghosts and quite another thing to see them."

Hear someone *talk about* ghosts…?

"I thought she might frighten him. Or bore him." Zashil laughed.

Faine and I exchanged a glance. "Zashil, did you tell Fred *all* about Luna Lane?" I asked.

Before he could answer, a man with an orange tan and greasy, slicked-back golden hair rounded the corner. "Not bad, not bad," he said, strolling up behind Zashil. His eyes flit to Faine appraisingly, pausing a beat too long at the way her curves filled out her vintage 1940s-style polka dot housedress.

The purple color popped against her pale skin and dark brown, wavy hair, her red lipstick and dark eyeshadow completing the pin-up beauty look. That didn't mean I wanted this guy who dripped sleaze appreciating her *that* closely.

"Is this the witch?" he asked, his eyes not moving from Faine.

Bananaberries. *Zashil, what have you done?*

Chapter Four

"*A* witch? Me? No," said Faine, nervous laughter escaping from between her lips. She looked at me out of the corner of her eye, whether to indicate I was the person he was looking for or to plead for my help, I couldn't be sure.

I wasn't wearing my witch hat. Maybe I should have been. That would have made it obvious.

I turned my gaze on Zashil, and he flinched but said nothing.

"Ah, so it must be you." Fred turned those leering eyes on me now and gave a little nod as he shifted from head to toe, as if to decide I'd do. For what, who could say?

Whatever it was, I was certain I wouldn't enjoy it.

I put a hand on my hip and straightened my back. "Why, might I ask, are you asking questions about witches?"

Fred readjusted the lapel of his flashy light blue suit. It clashed awfully with his tanned skin, and it seemed one size too large. "No offense, miss. To tell you the truth, I didn't believe him at first, but well, Zashil's good people." His eyes scanned the window behind me, landing on the mummy mayor wearing a suit but still wrapped in bandages. "And I've seen things. Just walking these streets, let me tell you…" He smiled at me, his eyes sparkling. "But you know that. You live here in this town of miracles."

Grabbing Zashil by the arm, I yanked him down the sidewalk a little. "You *told him*? Have your wits left you?"

He fumbled out of my grip and tugged at his checkered shirt sleeve. "Relax, Dahlia. Plenty of normies know about Luna Lane. Case in point." He gestured at himself.

"Yeah, the ones who live here! The ones who've been vetted!" Gazing over my childhood friend's shoulder, I found Faine with the fakest smile on her face taking careful steps toward the front door of her café as Fred pressed nearer and nearer to her with each rambling sentence he uttered. Whatever I had to say to Zashil, it'd have to be fast.

"Mom told me you even let a *visiting* professor in on the secret," he said, emphasizing the word "visiting." Of course Goldie would tell him about Cable. "It's not like Fred plans to move here—he's the franchisor—but he'll at least have roots here once we get this business up and running."

"Cable is Milton's family, and besides, he's known about Luna Lane since we were kids."

A hint of recognition flitted over his face. "Cable? Little scaredy cat Cable Woodward?"

So *he* remembered him right away.

"You weren't the bravest boy on the block, either," I said, huffing. I crossed my arms over my chest, relieved to see Grady step out from Hungry Like a Pup and wedge himself between Faine and Fred, the latter of whom had managed to lean an arm against the glass to hover over the rather petite Faine. He stepped back and shook Grady's hand, and I saw with disappointment he'd not only invaded my best friend's personal space, he'd left a handprint on the freshly cleaned glass. I growled, but from the stern slope of Grady's dark brow, it was clear he was doing all the menacing for me.

Zashil, following my gaze, took notice of the wrong things entirely. "Grady moved to Luna Lane, helped Faine open a business."

"Grady was her fiancé. And a fellow werewolf!" Just as vampires also existed in Transylvania and across the globe, so too did werewolves. It wasn't like they'd sprouted out from Luna Lane's soil or anything. Grady hailed from a village of werewolves in northern Canada to which Faine's parents had retired.

Somewhere out there, there were other witches, too. But only one ever made a visit to Luna Lane.

"He won't tell anyone," said Zashil stubbornly.

There was a dot of sweat along his brow, but he seemed determined to squash any second thoughts that might nag at him. "He's floating me the cash for this. It's a no-risk opportunity I couldn't pass up."

As Grady gathered the bucket and sponges I'd been using and opened the door for his wife to step inside the café, I massaged my temple because now Fred hollered at us and sauntered down our way.

I didn't even want to start wondering what kind of deal Zashil had gotten himself into. Fred reeked of a loan shark who didn't exactly loan money out of the kindness of his heart. Almost as if to prove my point, he dipped a hand into his front shirt pocket and pulled out a toothpick, sticking it between his teeth and chewing on it as he neared.

"He gets more of the profits the first few years," said Zashil, as if justifying himself, though I hadn't asked any follow-up questions. "But I get a salary, and eventually, my co-owner's stake raises if I can meet certain financial goals."

Fred took the toothpick out of his mouth and used it to point at the sign reading, "First Taste," leading to the vampire-run pub connected to the town's café. "Hey, I know we said we could meet for a late lunch, but how about we grab a beer instead?" He squinted at the sign and I noticed the crow's feet, the slight sag to his neck skin that looked artificially pinned. So he was forty, maybe pushing fifty, though I'd pinned him to be in his thirties at most originally. He clearly took great care of his appearance, though I couldn't say I was a fan of the neon tone his artificial tan gave his skin. He even smelled a bit like yeast from this distance. Yuck.

"It's fine with me," said Zashil. He looked to me.

It took me a moment to realize they were both staring at me.

"I don't care where you go," I said quickly. "But, Zashil, I wanted to talk to you—"

"Great." Fred slipped an arm around me and I shuddered. In shock, I didn't even slip out of it, just let him direct me toward the pub. "Like I said, Zashil promised me I'd get to dine with a witch today."

My mouth gaped as I looked over my shoulder at the man I'd *thought* was one of my closest childhood friends. He put his palms together in front of his face apologetically but said nothing more.

What in the world…?

We were already inside First Taste, the waft of eerie mist that characterized the place hitting my face before I *finally* got the strength of mind to slip out from Fred's grip. I gave him the evil eye, but he seemed oblivious to it as he waved at Jamie behind the counter. Jamie was a normie for sure. A bronzed complexion with a hint of paler skin peeking out from under his short-sleeved shirt's tan line, short, wavy golden brown hair, and a tall, willowy frame. No fangs in sight. Day shift. No vampires present—

a blessing, considering I'd been avoiding Draven all month.

"Do we just sit wherever?" Fred asked. No one else was in the bar. Afternoon hours were sparsely attended generally.

"Sure." Jamie looked to Fred, to me, to Zashil, then back to me. I supposed I was the only familiar face to him. I shrugged and followed Fred to a booth in the corner.

But only because I needed to talk some sense into Zashil before he let this obvious conman take him to the cleaners.

"I'll have a draft," Fred practically shouted across the room to Jamie. I supposed he had an excuse since the sound effects pumping through the pub's speakers included the low rumbling of thunder. But I still didn't like him any for it. "Zash?"

"Same," said Zashil, nearly sinking into his seat.

"*Zash?*" I muttered.

"And for the lady?" Fred asked.

"Seltzer water," I said quickly. Like I was going to pal around and have a beer with these two just then.

"Boy, they sure do know atmosphere," said Fred. He nudged Zashil in the arm. "Do we have some competition for spookiness or is this some Halloween theme for the month?"

I took in the setting of the bar. With the mist, the thunder, the painting of the old Transylvania village and castles on the walls, it was a tribute to the spooky homeland the vampires had left behind.

"It's this way year-round," I spat, crossing my arms and sinking into the booth across from Zashil. Maybe the "competition" would scare Fred away.

"You weren't wrong that this would be a hot spot for an escape room," said Fred, chuckling.

Great. I'd just made him even more determined to stay.

Jamie brought our drinks and stood a bit awkwardly, taking in the two who were strangers to him. "Anything else I can get you?"

"No, son, but let me introduce myself. Fred Beauchamp." He reached up over my head to grab Jamie's hand and shook it rather forcefully. Their elbows practically grazed my head. "You might know Zashil?"

"Jamie moved in after he left," I said. "Zashil is Goldie and Arjun's son."

"Oh!" Jamie's face lit up then. A little sense of familiarity. "Nice to meet you."

Zashil nodded, but Fred was determined to do all the speaking, apparently. "We're opening up an escape room in the old bowling alley. Drop by opening week and tell them Fred sent you." He winked. "Good for five percent off."

Oh, gee. A whole five percent.

"Escape room?" Jamie tucked his tray under his arm and leaned on the back of my booth seat. I could tell from his posture he was already intrigued.

"Yessiree," said Fred, relaxing back into his booth. "You tell all your friends, spread the word. Spooky Escape Rooms coming to Luna Lane!"

Jamie laughed. "Awesome! I've driven out to the next few counties over and done a few, but I never imagined one in Luna Lane. You hiring?"

I gazed up and met Jamie's eyes. "Are you leaving First Taste?"

He shrugged and stepped back. There was no mistaking the two round scars on his jugular vein. There were no bags under his eyes, though, so at least I knew Qarinah and Draven were being careful not to drag anyone to the brink of vampire venom addiction. "I don't know. I thought I could be a gamemaster part-time or something." His voice got quieter toward the end.

Draven wouldn't take well to someone like Fred poaching his day staff. And frankly, no matter what had gone on between Draven and me, neither would I.

"Ha, well, that's putting the cart before the horse just yet, but you keep in touch with Zash here. He's going to be in charge of the day-to-day."

Zashil pulled his wallet out of his back pocket and handed Jamie a business card. Clearly delighted, Jamie thanked him and headed back to the bar.

The list of complaints I had to register with my railroaded friend was going to take me all day.

"So," said Fred, popping the top and sipping the

foam off the top of his beer stein. "Hmm." He paused, gazing at his beer. "Old school. I like it. I love this place." He shook Zashil by the shoulder.

"About that——" I started.

Fred turned back to me as if I hadn't spoken. "Zashil told me he had a *very* interesting friend back home. A witch."

I ran a finger over the cold condensation clinging to my glass. "So I see. Not something I'd recommend he tell just *anyone*, but——"

"And I said, you're pulling my leg," Fred continued. He cackled and Zashil chuckled, too, just a beat too late for it to be spontaneous. "But then again, I spent some time in Creekdale when I was younger. I heard the rumors about ghosts and ghoulies over in Luna Lane." So there were rumors about us in the next town over? "I mean, no one actually believes it, but we don't go running over to tour the town much, either, you know? Just in case." He chortled. "So I said, you know what? Count me in. And now that I've toured the town, seen the sights, been shown all those fairy tales are true—this is the perfect place for a branch of my escape room."

"You *say* that, but I actually have to object." I turned my gaze on Zashil specifically. "You don't have a large enough customer base for something like an escape room here, and I don't know how the townspeople would feel about attracting loads of visitors. If there are rumors about us already in Creckdale—"

"Oh, you'll all reap the benefits," said Fred, fluffing it off. "More business for the café, the pub, all the little stores around here." The corner of his lips quirked up, unnaturally stretching his smile over those gleaming teeth. "I met quite a number running that tailor's shop. Had to step in and buy some threads. She seemed *quite* excited at the prospect of more business."

Spindra the spiderwoman. Fred was lucky she hadn't decided to Black Widow him like her kind were known to, despite her vow to do no harm when she'd moved into town.

Obliviousness. Sheer ignorance when it came to how dangerous the citizens of Luna Lane could truly be. Add a bunch of tourists into the mix and…

"I spoke to Mayor Abdel," said Zashil, finally piping up. "There isn't any lodging in town—"

"Tell me about it." Fred snorted. "He's got me holed up in his parents' guest room. Dinky little thing. And with him and Javi there, it's quite the crowded little place."

"My parents gave you their room," said Zashil, and if I wasn't wrong, his features tightened, like his business partner was finally starting to irritate him. "Javier and I are in my brother's and my old room. Mom and Dad are on the fold-out in the living room."

That was such a Goldie and Arjun thing to do. And for such an undeserving specimen.

"But an escape room is really a day trip destination," continued Zashil, clearing his throat. "We think they'd swing by, stop for lunch or a drink, maybe a little shopping, and be on their way."

I frowned. "And Mayor Abdel was fine with this?"

"Who wouldn't be?" Fred slammed his palms against the table, though it was more in excitement than anger.

I let a breath escape my lips. They made it seem so reasonable on the surface. Day trips might be doable. In and out, and nothing much to see here, other than a spooky theme bar and maybe an eccentric mayor and a ghastly pale Victorian-era woman if she managed to stay corporeal whenever any stranger was around.

Oh, I knew Virginia couldn't be counted on for that.

"I still don't like it," I said, taking a quick sip of my drink. "What about the construction workers, for one? Where are they going to stay? How are they going to not notice the town's… unique flavor?"

"I like that." Fred beamed and pointed a thumb at me, turning to Zashil. "Get her advice on some marketing."

I shook my head. "No… I don't… You're not answering the question."

"Ah, but that's where you come in, sweetheart." Fred finished off his beer and pushed it aside so he could lean both arms on the table, practically bursting at the seam to tell me the news.

Again, he'd railroaded me before I could complain that I certainly wasn't his "sweetheart" or any such term of endearment.

"When Zash told me he was struggling to gather enough capital for his share of the location, he pitched an incredible way we could save on construction expenses."

"Zashil…?" I said, not liking where this was going.

"I was going to ask her—" started Zashil, but Fred butted in again.

"We task the local witch, his old friend, the town's most benevolent do-gooder, as he tells me, with building our escape room in a day."

Chapter Five

*T*here was so much wrong with everything he'd just said.

Task me, not ask me or hire me? In a day?

Oh, and *me*? Why in the world would I even do such a thing?

"I wash windows. I stock shelves," I sputtered, barely even knowing where to start. "I don't build buildings."

"I've seen you create a tree out of a bush," Zashil said with a fixed gaze and a reverent voice. He was doing a darn good job of painting me like some eighth wonder of the world.

"That was…" I thought back to it, just some fooling around I'd done as a kid. "I don't know. I didn't know what I was doing. I was taking some-thing to make something else, not conjuring a miracle out of thin air."

"You wouldn't be creating something out of

nothing." Fred leaned back, his confidence not in the least bit shaken. "There's the broken-down bowling alley, plenty of parts to futz around with in there. And we had a delivery this morning. Don't worry," he said before I could object to delivery people stopping by. "It was a quick in-and-out job, and the guys are long gone. All the real technical parts we make at our warehouse to ship out to our locations. We have a stack of them ready to go. Though if you think you can create these parts out of dirt or garbage or something, it'd be a great way to save some cash—"

"No," I told him flatly.

"Shame. We could have made you our one-woman parts warehouse from here on out."

I wasn't sure he was joking.

He leaned forward to pull a smartphone out of his pocket and swiped the screen a few times. "Blue-prints are in here. I've used these designs at half a dozen other franchise locations. They're solid, tested —quite easy to replicate for a witch of your caliber."

A witch of my caliber? As if the man had anyone else to compare me to.

"I can't." My eyes flitted against my will over the images he scrolled through as he held the phone out to me. A bunch of blue backgrounds and white lines I couldn't begin to understand if my life depended on it.

"You can," said Zashil, reaching across the table

to take hold of my hand.

Fred shrugged and placed his phone on the table in front of him. "If you don't, that means figuring out the logistics of getting the workers here and finding them places to stay. An extra expense in the tens of thousands that'll take us *years* to recoup, if we ever do." Fred fidgeted with his hands. "This place is perfect, Miss—oh my goodness, I never got your name."

Yeah. There was that strike against him, too.

"Dahlia," I muttered, pulling my hand back to my lap. "Dahlia Poplar."

"Miss Poplar, you're right. A small town is a bit risky, though you'd be surprised where I've opened locations before—sometimes the smallest towns are itching the most for something to *do*." He chortled and I bristled. There was plenty to do in Luna Lane. "Change up the rooms every year or so, and you get the same clientele in the bag, expand to new people with every new room—the place really sustains itself. But you know what's the biggest expense, after that initial property purchase or rental? Construction. Initial construction, pulling down the rooms that have run their course, putting up new ones…" He tapped his phone. "My architect and I, we've done all the designing. We space our locations just far enough away from one another that it doesn't matter too much that we recycle designs—we're far from the only name in the business that does this. But a witch—a witch who can reshape a room with the wave of her wand, that… That's something incredible, Miss Poplar. That's something I would *kill* to be able to do."

"I don't use a wand," I muttered, downing the last of my glass.

Fred's lips grew tight, as if fighting back a smile. "However you work your magic, then. I'm prepared to offer you a reasonable price for your services."

No doubt way less than he'd offer any construction crew. "I don't need money," I said. It was true. Mom's extra-dimensional vault never seemed to run out of cash.

Fred frowned. "Well, Zash here told me you *had* to help people? Some kind of curse or something?" His leering eyes stopped over my exposed forearm and the stone scales. I covered them as best I could with my right hand out of instinct.

"Tell him my whole life story, why don't you?" I slung at Zashil. Everything but my *name*.

Zashil winced. "Sorry, I just—he's willing to take on all the financial risk because I thought you might help us out, Dahlia. Please. I could never afford something like this otherwise."

"Your parents might lend you—"

Zashil shook his head. "I wouldn't risk their money. I couldn't. They work too hard, and it's not like they've got a lot to spare. They spoil my niece and nephew too much."

That sounded a lot like them.

"Well," I said, tapping my fingers on the table.

"You've got one thing wrong. Not that I expect you to understand the minutiae of said *curse*, but what you're asking for—that wouldn't help me with it. At all." I rounded on Zashil. "Good deeds only count if I don't rely too heavily on magic, remember?"

Zashil slouched in his seat. "Right. I forgot about that."

"Then forget about this good deed curse or whatever," said Fred, brushing aside the focal point of my life like it were no more than an annoying gnat. "Let's cut to the chase. You have the ability to do this. Zashil talked you up quite highly. What's it going to take to convince you?"

I was glad *someone* had faith in my abilities.

Okay, then. Why consider doing this? *How* to do this?

It wasn't like I'd be making something out of nothing.

I had my witch's hat, and I could easily brew a number of potions to boost my magical energy.

I'd wanted to practice the bigger spells more.

I wouldn't be *designing* anything. I didn't have to know the ins and outs of the puzzles and traps or whatever made an escape room come together. I just had to make those blueprints a reality.

"Unless you can conjure up some cash, a bunch of tents for the workers to stay in, and wipe their memories after they leave town?" Fred ventured. He added a chuckle belatedly, like maybe he hoped I'd jump in and say I could do just that.

Memory wiping. I'd always been too afraid to try it. It was too easy to get wrong, to hurt someone.

It was a spell Eithne had used countless times before.

I couldn't do that.

We couldn't have those construction workers here for weeks, for months on end—and apparently coming back at least once a year to change up the room design.

"Okay," I said, lifting my hands up in surrender. "If everyone else in town is open to this, I'll give it a try."

"Excellent!" said Fred, clapping his hands together. He reached over and practically snatched my arm up to shake my hand. "You won't regret this, Della. I promise you. You'll see. A Spooky Escape Rooms location is just what your tiny little town needs. Bartender? Another round?" he shouted over my shoulder, practically shattering an eardrum.

I was regretting this already.

"It's Dahlia," said Zashil softly. Fred didn't seem to hear him. But Zashil was looking straight at me, his eyes sparkling. "Thank you, Dahlia. For making my dream come true."

His *dream*, huh?

Well, what was the worst that could happen? I'd fixed the little disaster with Cable in the garden no problem.

I'd fix any little issues that came up if need be.

Chapter Six

"*E*nchanting an escape room into existence, huh? That doesn't seem like something you'd throw yourself into."

Sherriff Roan eyed me over the top of his beer bottle. A bit paunchy, the sole policeman of Luna Lane wore his sheriff's uniform to the pub after work, though his hat was conspicuously absent over his nearly bald head.

"I've wanted to practice something big for a while now anyway," I said. "Maybe it's not just a matter of the right potion. Eithne can do anything. My mom could do more than me. If I get strong enough, I can—"

"Turn hair into hats and flesh into gloves?" Roan said wryly. He grinned and took another sip of his beer. "Sorry. Couldn't resist. Whole town's heard about that."

My cheeks flushed as I tapped the stem of my

margarita glass. It was only my second, and it would be my last. I had a buzz going in my head, but I needed it clear for a good night's sleep.

I just also needed something to take the edge off if I was going to get said night's sleep at all.

"That's exactly why I need to practice with these types of things," I said softly. I should have known I couldn't count on even Cable to keep anything quiet in a small town.

Roan, who'd always been just shy of the father I'd never had growing up, the "uncle" who'd stopped by to make sure my mom and I had had everything we'd needed, studied me with those detective eyes of his and seemed to get at what was really bothering me.

"Cable only told us because he was worried you'd overexerted yourself," he explained. "When you passed out yesterday morning."

"That was from pain, not from expending too much magic. I've never *passed out* from using magic."

"You've never used a large amount of it before," Roan pointed out.

With shaky hands, I took another sip.

Back at the booth, Fred's noxious laughter rang out, his words flitting in and out, as it seemed he was regaling the Mahajans with some kind of story about a group of escape room customers who'd mooned the cameras they'd known had been watching them during their game.

Goldie's laughter was infectious, though I detected a twinge of nervousness to it.

I wondered what time it was. After Fred had worn my ear off with explanations of every little detail of the escape room construction plans, I'd dragged my feet next door to Hungry Like a Pup for dinner. Faine had warily shown muted enthusiasm for the task I'd set for myself and my confidence had waned even more. She'd excused herself to deliver dinner for Milton and Cable—I supposed that meant he was back from his errand out of town, must have been so nice to be able to get out of town —and I'd wandered back into the pub for a little bit of something to ease my nerves.

Broomie leaned against the bar between Roan and me, her nap disturbed every few moments by a roar of recorded thunder or another of Fred's grating cackles.

"I should get back," I said, sliding off the stool. Now that I thought about it, if Roan had joined me, that meant it was after work, close to sundown. "It's too noisy in here for Broomhilde."

But Zashil and his family and Fred seemed to be having the same idea at just the same time. The chairs that Jamie had dragged over to Fred's booth so Goldie, Arjun, and Javier could join them scraped backward against the linoleum floor.

I quickly took my seat at the bar again.

Roan arched an eyebrow but said nothing. The

conversation—dominated by Fred, of course—grew louder as the group made its way by.

"Dahlia, dear, I'm so glad to see you're better." Goldie appeared at my side, readjusting her purse strap over her arm.

I squeezed her hand. "I am, thank you. And I'm so sorry."

"*We* should be sorry," said Arjun, slipping in beside his wife.

"Of course you shouldn't be," I said. "I was foolish, that's all. And it was an easy fix once I woke up. Thank you all for worrying about me, and for the food—it was delicious. I'll have to bring the dish by later."

"Don't worry about it. It was the least I could do —and Zashil tells us you're helping with the escape room?"

Fred didn't let either of Zashil's parents breaking away from him stop him from talking. Javier, Zashil's husband, was the sole focus of the man's drivel now. Javier, short and muscular, stood his own against the man's dominating presence, offering a friendly, if tight, smile and leaning forward into the space Fred was trying to invade. With his buzz cut, complete with abstract patterns crafted into the fuzz, and his trim facial hair, it was easy to see why my childhood friend had fallen for him.

I sent him a flittering smile, wondering if he knew I could tell what he was doing. His eyes sparkled as they landed on me for just a second before his attention turned back to Fred, whom he wouldn't let drop him out of the conversation entirely. "Have you ever had to call security on customers like that?" Javier asked, speaking over Fred.

Fred didn't seem the least bit fazed. "Oh, no. No one's really pushed things that far. Drunks are our biggest problem. That and idiots who can't follow simple directions. But it's not like they *mean* to cause damage."

Roan and Arjun were talking now, and all the conversation buzzing around me was getting to my head.

"Yes," I said to Goldie, wincing as a headache started raging. "Apparently, I'm building it. In a day."

Goldie's brow furrowed. "Are you up for such a task?"

I waved her off, the buzz of the drink maybe making me a tad too tipsy. "Everyone keeps telling me that. I'm fine. The worst that could happen is I fail and they have to bring in outside workers for a few weeks." I took the last sip of my drink. It was still cold and it tingled against my tongue.

I jumped as all of a sudden two heavy hands clamped down on my shoulders. Fred's breath was hot over the top of my head, and it smelled strongly of peppermint.

"I don't *like to* cut corners, but I always make

sure to look into every way to save money. If only I could bring this miraculous witch you have here with me to every location of Spooky Escape Rooms! We'd make a mint!"

Flinching, I tried rolling my shoulders out of his grip, keeping my eyes focused on the empty margarita glass in front of me. "I haven't even succeeded yet."

"You will. Mark my words: You will." He squeezed my shoulders harder.

"You're crowding the lady. Please step back."

That voice had several effects.

It made Fred drop my shoulders immediately and take a few steps back.

It made all the conversation in the bar die out entirely.

And it sent a spine-tingling shiver throughout my entire body.

I looked up. Behind the counter was Draven, vampire proprietor of First Taste, Gothic-style fetching in black leather clashing with his long, blond hair, and my ex-boyfriend.

Qarinah, the other vampire in town and co-owner, was at the end of the bar, discussing shift changeover business with Jamie.

That meant the sun was down.

Bananaberries. I'd meant to be home before this happened.

Fred didn't seem *too* daunted by Draven's steely gray gaze. He leaned in between Roan and me and extended his hand toward the glowering vampire. "You must be Draven? Fred Beauchamp. Going to open the escape room in town with your home-grown son here, Zash."

Rather than shake the man's hand, Draven crossed his arms and leaned back. The slight tug on his open leather jacket revealed more of his glistening white pecs.

Fred grimaced just the tiniest bit and pulled his hand back, smoothly running it across the sleek stubble on his cheek. "Excellent atmosphere. Just the kind of place an escape room should have a deal with." He turned to Zashil. "What do you think, Zash? Some kind of coupon exchange?"

Zashil shrugged. "Sure."

Roan swiveled on his seat. "Maybe we should make sure it's up and running before we discuss cross-promotion and the like, don't you think?"

Fred glowered at Roan. "I'm sorry. Have we been introduced?"

"Roan Birch." The sheriff offered Fred his right hand, after transferring his beer to his left. "Local law enforcement. Might need to let me know about those drunks and mischief makers you expect at your establishment?"

"Oh, it's nothing, I assure you." Fred took Roan's hand gladly. "But I'd be happy to have a chat. Maybe tomorrow? We need to make sure all those licenses are approved and building codes are

74

adhered to. Do we get to skip over those in an extraordinary town like Luna Lane?"

"Well," said Roan, slipping off his stool. He put his empty bottle down and exchanged a knowing look with Qarinah at the end of the bar. Her gorgeous face lit up with a warm smile, her red-rimmed dark eyes practically drinking him in from across the room. "Not typically, no," Roan said, turning back to Fred. "But I'll take a look at what you've started with town hall since the sale of the property."

"Surely, if a witch can build our business in a day, the red tape that plagues the small business owner in any other community could be... *bent* a little."

Their conversation got quieter as the two headed for the door. Licking his lips, Fred kept shifting his gaze every few seconds to Qarinah, voluptuous and with a perfect wan, brown complexion and silky, black hair. It was easy to see why a natural seductress would catch his eye, though she only had eyes for Roan.

If Fred got lucky, she might let him be supper someday. The thought of her shutting him up by sinking her fangs into his jugular made me giggle for a moment.

"What's so funny?" snapped Draven.

"Ah," said Arjun, suddenly jumpy. "We should get back then. Tomorrow's a big day. Thank you again, Dahlia, for helping out our son."

"A big day," I concurred, lifting my empty glass up and offering a toast.

Broomie cooed from beside me and crawled up onto the stool Roan had vacated. Javier gave her a little pat and she leaned up into his touch.

"Thank you, Dahlia." Zashil took both my hands in his, swinging me around. I almost fell of the stool. "Honestly, I'm going to owe you for life."

"If it works," I reiterated.

"It will." He slipped an arm around his husband and they both bade me goodnight, Goldie and Arjun on their tails—after Goldie fussed over my health just a bit more and made sure to pet Broomhilde.

The bar was so much emptier once they'd all exited. Jeremiah the farmer was off in a booth with one of his farmhands and Jamie and Qarinah spoke in quiet tones about the business of the day.

Draven's oppressive glare was tangible. I practically sunk into my seat.

"Since when do you let obnoxious men fondle you like that?" he snapped.

I bristled. I hadn't liked Fred's touch, that was for certain, but I suddenly felt on the defensive. "He wasn't *fondling* me." The world was tilting just a little and I gripped the bar to steady myself.

"I beg to differ." He *tsked*. "Why are you drinking? You could never handle your liquor."

Another low blow. "I had two margaritas!"

"One too many, apparently." He snatched the

empty glass from in front of me, little flakes of salt shaking off from the rim and peppering the counter.

"You're mean," I said, my voice slurring just a bit. It was juvenile, but it was true.

He sighed and released the empty glass into a basin behind him, his reflection shimmery and unfocused in the small wall mirror above the basin. Contrary to popular belief, vampires weren't entirely invisible in mirrors and they did manage to show up in pictures. I wished they didn't, though, because I'd had to spend too long during a low point in the breakup sorting through the stack of them we'd taken as a couple before tossing them into the fireplace and watching them burn to ash.

I stared at Draven as he busied himself with pretend tasks, his reflection a strange blur that made me wonder if I was hallucinating. Good thing Cable had never come in here back when I'd been worried about him discovering the truth about Luna Lane. That reminded me. How were we going to keep the "day trip" visitors from noticing the nightshift at the bar had no clear reflections?

Another problem to add to the mountain of them.

Zashil had looked so happy when he'd thanked me. I didn't want to crush his dreams—and he was going to find a way to get this done, with or without me.

Finally, after a moment of silence, the blond

vampire spun back to face me. "Dahlia, Faine told me you're planning on building an escape room in a day with your enchantments? Can you handle such a thing?"

"Why does everyone keep doubting me?" And talking about me behind my back. Faine must have poured out the whole sordid story about Fred and Zashil and me when restocking the pub's bar snacks with Draven before Hungry Like a Pup shuttered for the day.

"I'm not doubting you." Draven leaned on the counter, his face uncomfortably close to my own. His neck was stiff, his muscles strained. "I'm worried about you."

I slid off my stool, my black ballet slippers touching the floor. "I'm fine." I stumbled a little and caught myself. Without thinking, I pointed both hands at myself. "KNURD SSEL," was what I'd meant to say—I wanted a little buzz to go to sleep better. But I had no idea what words came out of my mouth.

The wash of magic slammed against me like a little one-two punch of air.

"Dahlia!" Draven popped into bat form with a crack, flew over the counter, then popped back into the icy cold, handsome man who leaned behind me, stopping me from toppling over entirely.

I giggled. "You squeaked. Like a little mouse." I squeaked and squeaked in imitation of cute little batty him.

"I'm taking you home," he said sternly.

Broomie unfurled herself, standing up straight and nudging between us. *Thatta girl.*

"She's got me," I said, gripping on to her shaft. "Were there always two handles?" I asked clumsily, trying to grip whichever one was real. Broomie bristled, indignant, nudging her handle herself into my other hand.

For a man who didn't breathe, a lot of air kept escaping from between those tight lips.

"Slap me," he said. "Punch me. Whatever you have to do—but stop hating me, Dahlia. I can't stand it."

That had taken a turn fast. "I'm… zorry?" I slurred. Broomie, the good girl, pushed me up as I spun around, making sure I didn't topple over entirely.

"I want us to at least be friends," he said softly. He looked so cute. I wanted to pinch his pale cheek and for some reason, before I could think too hard about it, I found myself doing exactly that.

"You're so adorable when you're sad," I said, not even realizing at first I'd said it aloud.

Covering my hand in his, he flattened it against his cheek. His skin was icy, but the part of my wrist where a stone scale was absorbed the cold, embraced it, like a desert traveler parched for water.

I couldn't focus my thoughts. "What did you pay?" I said quietly. There was something I'd zeroed in on.

"What?" he asked, confusion dotting his face. He didn't move my hand away.

"For the cursed game. You told me most people wouldn't pay Eithne's price."

He chewed his lip, the tip of one of his fangs poking outward. "A kiss," he said softly.

I cackled, the sound obnoxious even to my ears. "You're joking." I pulled my hand away, gripping Broomie with both hands like she were a handlebar keeping me upright on unsteady legs. She kept trilling as she attempted to keep me upright.

"I'm not." He shrugged. "It meant nothing to me, so I didn't think much of it."

I found myself tracing his lips with one index finger. "What did an evil witch want with these lips?" My voice was throaty, husky even.

"I didn't know," he said, his lips tickling my fingertip. "I thought she was merely toying with me."

I frowned. My heart beat so loudly in my ears, and my fingers slipped away.

Eithne had toyed with a vampire—*my* vampire —for a kiss. Had she watched me date him, felt anything like jealousy? Or had it just been her playing around, like he'd said? "So what did she ask Ravana for?" I asked. Ravana, Draven's sire, had been beautiful, too. Had she tempted Eithne in a similar way?

"I didn't know, but we got word from Transylvania today. I wanted to tell you before anyone else

—and then I found you here, in my pub, where I'd never have expected you." He paused, watching me, considering, maybe, how to proceed. "She was tried there for her crimes in spreading blood madness, for which she was sentenced to a hundred year's confinement"—he stumbled a little on his words then, and I wondered if he still felt some affection for his sire, but he recovered quickly—"and it came out. For Eithne's help in manipulating the memories of Luna Lane's citizens over a number of decades, Ravana paid with vampire venom in its purest, most distilled form—straight from the fang."

I didn't like the sound of that.

"What could she do with vampire venom?" I posited. "Drive someone blood mad?"

"Perhaps, though it'd be through some other means than is typical, as venom addiction usually comes about while a vampire is drinking blood." He winced. "She could have done any number of things, Dahlia. Vampire venom has been used in witches' brews for hundreds of years for countless reasons—but there's always one very important common thread."

It was like he'd splashed my face with water, snapping the drunk right out of me. I'd read it before… Vampire venom, listed in ingredients. I'd never attempted any of those potions. There hadn't been a need to. "What kind of thread?"

"Vampire venom is usually a necessary ingre-dient in a curse."

Chapter Seven

I'd used a quick, simple enchantment to banish all traces of a hangover this morning, but there was still nothing like the smooth, black brew of Faine's morning coffee to help settle my jittery nerves.

Could I use an enchantment to calm myself? Maybe. I'd never bothered before. Not a lot in Luna Lane made me as anxious as the thought of reshaping an entire building to meet very specific specifications despite never attempting such a feat before.

And there was that *other thing* weighing on my mind. To curse me before birth, Eithne might have used Ravana's venom somehow. Yet another reason why I was glad that murderous vampire was out of town for good.

But now that I knew what had likely been a key ingredient in the curse Eithne had crafted for me in what was supposed to have been the warm succor of my mother's belly, I might have a better shot at counteracting it.

If I became a stronger witch who could take on tasks like the one I'd set for myself today.

The coffee was bold, strong, and *hot* against my quite-sore tongue. At least it washed away the taste of pine needles and dirt and other unsavory ingredients from the two power-boosting potions I'd choked down this morning.

Faine bounced in place beside me. She had on a classy wool coat over her dress, whereas I had put on a shawl over my dress and my witch's hat on my head and had called it a day. It *was* getting chillier and chillier these days, but I usually enchanted myself to feel warmer if it bothered me.

Now I was too nervous to enchant an ant to pick up a crumb—which it would likely have attempted to do anyway.

"Thanks for coming," I said to Faine, gripping her by the mitten and squeezing.

She squeezed back. "Of course! The kids wanted to come, but the girls had school and Grady kept Falcon back with him at the café. We decided he could do without too much *excitement* for a while."

Couldn't we all?

I stared at the empty bowling alley in front of me. The boarded-up window covered up most of my view of the inside, but I could still see through the slats and the glass door. There was a stack of things that hadn't been there last month, freshly delivered escape room parts and pieces that Fred had assured me would make my job easier.

"Good morning, ladies."

The chipper, deep voice was unexpected—but most welcome.

"If you can call it *that*," added a high-pitched voice I also hadn't been expecting. "A bit overcast, don't you think? Might it rain?"

Faine shivered beside me. "Storms weren't on the forecast." She kept up with that since they agitated her wolf side.

This conversation hung heavily in my already roiling stomach. It was all too familiar.

"Cable, Virginia," I said, turning to the two friends who'd shown up, I supposed, for moral support.

Cable looked like he'd stepped out of a clothes magazine for fashionable fall attire. Everything from his wire-rimmed glasses to his long, tan trench coat and red plaid scarf looked picture perfect. He handed me a little white paper bag.

"What's this?" I asked curiously, taking it from him. Faine grabbed my empty coffee cup so I could inspect it closer and I thanked her for tossing it out for me.

"I drove into the city yesterday," he said. "I wasn't sure when you'd wake up from your injury, and I'm sorry I missed you, but I thought you could use this when you got back."

Broomhilde soared over from wherever she'd been zooming about nearby, hovering next to the floating Virginia, both poking their figurative noses over my shoulder to get a closer look.

Inside was a wedge-like package containing some kind of snack. The tan label described it as "oatcakes." "What's this?"

"Traditional Scottish oatcakes. It's a favorite of mine back home. I didn't expect Goldie and Arjun to stock it and waiting on Amazon delivery seemed a bit iffy—"

Ripping open the package, I inhaled. It smelled… cozy. "It smells great. But why?" I reached in and popped the first one in my mouth. Virginia licked her lips and I felt bad she couldn't try any, but I offered one to Faine. She took one and chewed it slowly, her chef instincts kicking in, no doubt, to analyze the new food.

"Well, I…" Cable's cheeks darkened. "I didn't know how to help you. You had Doc Day, and everyone assured me your magic would take care of the injury once you awoke, so what could I do?"

"I'd say you did rather a lot." The back of my neck felt suddenly flush with sweat. "Virginia told me you carried me home."

Cable's teeth were brilliant when he smiled. "That was the least I could do."

"Well, I disagree. Thank you." I took another one of the snacks. A little plain, but it had just the right amount of sweetness. "This is good. Thank you again. But—"

"Why food?" He rubbed the back of his head, his elbow poking out at an awkward angle. "It comforted me back home when I was getting used to living alone, to having roots in one place. I just wanted to share a little comfort with you."

Silence settled in the air between us, the slight rustle of the leaves of trees down the block the only sound. I felt antsy under his gaze, but I wouldn't have broken it for the world.

"I bet it's better than that haggis," said Virginia plainly, interrupting the moment.

Clearing my throat, I rolled the top of the bag shut. My nerves were too rattled for much food, though the tasty snack *was* having something of a calming effect on me.

Or maybe it was just the mood.

"So? What'd I miss yesterday?" Cable asked, taking in the bowling alley in front of us. "Virginia told me you're taking on construction now?"

"It's all *anybody's* talking about." Virginia hovered up and down in excitement, a peculiar, kind of determined look on her face. That explained how she'd found out about it in the first place. "Mr. Zashil Mahajan's new business, Miss Poplar being a champ and putting it together with an enchantment —*oh*, we just have to play a round as Spooky Games Club, don't you think?"

A small tittering sound escaped my lips. I'd been

so focused on crafting the darn thing that I hadn't thought that far ahead, but yeah, of course these Games Club devotees would want to try on an escape room for size. Goldie had said the same thing.

To tell the truth, even I was a bit excited now. I'd seen them on TV, but I'd never imagined one would open in our sleepy town. Though I still wasn't positive it was the best idea.

"Dahlia, can you handle this?" asked Cable.

And there went my burgeoning, fickle enthusiasm.

Sighing, I handed the bag back to him. "Hold this and we'll see."

Virginia charged through the slats over the broken window, her green ectoplasm oozing down the wood.

"Morning!" called another familiar voice, but as I turned with a smile on my face to greet Sherriff Roan, it slipped quickly.

Half the town was here, walking down the block behind him.

Okay, that was an exaggeration, but how many people were here to witness my shame?

They spilled out into the road, even. Mayor Abdel, Chione, and the other two workers from town hall, Ryan and Erik. Doc Day was even walking arm-in-arm with a hobbling, wiry-haired Milton, and we were halfway across town from our houses. He'd gotten dressed up for this, his checkered shirt tucked into a belt atop his khaki pants. His wife's glasses still hung on a chain around his neck, looking a little out of place—but he so rarely wanted to part from them.

"Uncle!" said Cable warmly. "Out for a walk?"

"I told him about our Dahlia's project today, and he got so excited. Seemed very in the moment," said Doc Day. Since Milton had dementia, he wasn't always present enough to recognize what was going on around him.

Virginia popped her head out from the wooden slats with a slimy, suction-like sound. "There are all sorts of puzzle boxes and locks and things here, among the wood and bricks and other stuff." She stuck her hand out from the slats and waved it around excitedly. "I can't wait until this is all together!" Then, without waiting for another word, she vanished inside.

"Hello, Dahlia," said Milton with a broad smile.

"Hi, Milton," I said back, nervously digging my fingernails into my palms. He hadn't reacted to Virginia's phasing through a solid surface with any surprise, so it really did feel like he was entirely back with us for the moment.

Taking a deep breath, I surveyed the gathering crowd. The men I was waiting for weren't at the front of it.

"Hello, everyone," I said, my throat crackling. "I… I, uh, didn't expect to be putting on a show."

Rumbles and merriment went out among the

crowd of at least fifty gathered around me. Even Jamie was there—I supposed the pub wasn't open yet. Jeremiah had driven in from his farm on the outskirts long before usual. Spindra, the spider-woman, leaned against a streetlamp, black hair over half her face and her long, black dress clinging to every dimple in her sallow skin. As a creature of the night, she rarely chose to be out during the day, so seeing her here was quite a surprise. She was staring at Cable, who was speaking in low tones to his uncle and Doc Day. She'd met him at least once. I wondered how *that* had gone. Spiderwomen were not to be outdone by vampires when it came to seduction.

I took in the rest of the crowd and had to take a deep breath. Virginia really *had* gotten word around town. "Just don't… Don't get too close. And don't laugh if I fail."

Jamie cupped his hands over his lips. "You can do it, Dahlia!"

Faine squeezed my hand, ripping my nails away from crafting craters in my palm. "Just do your best, and it's okay," she said softly.

"Dahlia! Dahlia!" A chant of my name shifted outward among the crowd, Jamie leading the way as he raised a fist in the air.

Butterflies floated in my stomach, but I felt ready already.

"Now this is the kind of community spirit I like to hear!" Fred stepped out from behind Jamie, sparing a quick, lingering glance over Spindra before turning back to me. Spindra watched him with her silvery eye like a hawk about to pounce on its prey. But she looked at any halfway handsome man like that.

"Well, Dahlia," said Fred, getting my name right for once. "Are you ready?" He pulled his smartphone out of his pocket and tapped at the screen as he stood beside me.

There was a text he brushed away before he brought up the blueprints. I caught the words "URGENT. RETURN MY CALLS" before the preview of the message disappeared. I hadn't even paid attention to the sender's name.

I studied Fred for a moment, but he didn't seem the least bit bothered by the message.

"So, how do you think this should work? Give you one more study of the blueprints or…?" Behind him, Zashil and Javier finally caught up, Goldie and Arjun arm-in-arm to their side. They must have closed down Vogel's for this. They *never* closed down Vogel's during regular hours. Not even on Christmas.

No pressure, no pressure, I told myself.

I took one more breath and Faine dropped my hand, stepping back. Fred's gaze followed her movement and I straightened my back to block most of his view of her.

Creep was gonna be a creep, I supposed. Thank

goodness he wasn't planning on sticking around once this place got up and running.

"Just hold the phone out in front of me," I said. I'd thought hard about this, how best to transfer his tested vision to the building in front of me. He'd provided the pieces, the plan. Anything extra could be crafted out of the old broken-down parts of the bowling alley. It was just a matter of making his vision reality. I didn't need to think hard about every little detail.

Grounding my feet hard into the pavement, I stuck both arms out in front of me.

"Dahlia!" Faine cried just as I opened my mouth. "Virginia!"

Oh. Right. I was *not* going to unintentionally catch poor Virginia up in one of my enchantments again.

Sure, it had helped us crack the case of the cursed game, so to speak, but we weren't solving anything now.

And I didn't blame Virginia for being huffy about it.

"There's someone inside?" asked Fred. If it was actually possible with his bread-colored tan, I would have thought he'd gone a few shades paler.

"A ghost," I said plainly.

Fred let out what had to be a deliberately quiet exhale. Then he blinked. "A *ghost?*"

"Virginia?" I called out. "I need you to come back outside."

Nothing happened, so I opened the door leading inside.

"Ginny?"

Fred bristled belatedly, practically doing a double take. "A ghost? Do you think she might interfere with the operations?" Fred's voice was the quietest I'd ever heard it, almost reverent, as he leaned over my shoulder and peered inside. "That might make for some memorable experiences, but if we can't control the puzzle solving to a precise degree, the whole game is shot."

"Zashil will talk to her," I said dismissively. "He knows her."

"He knows a ghost…?" Fred grew louder then, chuckling. "A witch, a ghost, a vampire? Why not?"

We stepped inside the darkened bowling alley, being careful to step around the piles of wrapped lumber, electronics, and other parts and pieces Fred had had delivered once the sale of the building had gone through.

"Virginia?" Faine fell in behind us.

"I see you are wearing my suitcoat," said Spindra, her Slavic accent punctuating each word.

We all turned to her. She'd slipped inside behind Faine as quiet as an arachnid, her long, pale fingers with black-painted nails trailing up the side of Fred's coat.

Fred grinned as if he'd just won some kind of jackpot. "I am. It's so soft, I can hardly keep my fingers off it." He took her hand in his, running it over the material across his chest.

Oh, please. Get a room. Though Fred might not walk out of it, come to think.

"Virginia!" I called out.

After another five minutes of carefully walking through the dust and debris, the crowd growing inside the bowling alley to explore every nook and cranny and help call out her name, someone finally shouted from back outside on the sidewalk.

"Out here!"

It was Mayor Abdel. He waved a wrappings-covered hand at us from the doorway.

The crowd started filing out, but I was at the back of it. I startled when I passed what had once been the shoe rental counter and Spindra and Fred popped out from behind it. Fred's hair was mussed, his suitcoat halfway down his arm.

I leveled Spindra with a look. At a time like this, around all these people? Spiderwomen thrived on seduction, but…

"She was not down there," she said simply, sliding past me and sashaying her hips.

"Nope. No ghosts down there." Fred readjusted his suitcoat and smoothed down his greasy hair. His suitcoat *did* seem of better quality than the cheap thing he'd had on the day before, a smooth silk made of burgundy that didn't clash with his tan so much, and it fit him like a glove.

I scuttled away as quick as a mouse without a

word.

Outside, the crowd dispersed outward again, revealing Broomie flying in circles above Cable's, Milton's, Doc Day's—and Virginia's heads.

"Virginia, we've been *calling* for you," I said, approaching her. Broomie glided down beside me and did a quick cat-like loop around my legs. I patted her. She was acting so triumphant, she must have found our wayward ghost.

Virginia's feet were actually on the ground. She looked at me sharply and produced her parasol out of thin air again, leaning it against her shoulder and practically hiding behind it, letting the lace obscure half her face.

"I heard," she said simply.

"You heard…? And you just let us keep looking?"

"I'm *so sorry* making sure you didn't trap me in a locked box or something of the sort this time inconvenienced you," she snapped.

What was wrong with her?

"I take it this is the ghost we're looking for?" Fred was positively champing at the bit. He brushed past me, his arm clipping mine. "Fred Beauchamp," he said, his hand extended.

Virginia stuck her nose in the air and offered him just the slightest bit of her profile.

Fred wriggled his eyebrows. "I'm sorry if I offended you, miss. I don't suppose a ghost can shake a hand, can she?" His eyes narrowed as he attempted to lean around me to get a closer look. "I don't know what I expected… But you seem almost real, somehow. Pale, sure, but paleness seems to be a thing in this town." He looked over his shoulder at Spindra, who was between Chione and Mayor Abdel. She grinned widely and waved her fingers at him.

Virginia put a hand—a solid hand, though she strangely kept it in a fist, almost like she was clutching something—on Cable's shoulder and he jumped. Maybe she'd never touched him before, but I knew she felt cold, colder than a vampire. "I can touch what I please whenever I please," Virginia said simply, and then she lifted off the ground a couple of inches and floated down the block and away.

She never did like to be ignored or talked down to. I shivered. Like I had time just now to worry about her moods.

"That's a prude if I've ever seen one," muttered Fred. He clapped his hands beside me. "So everyone is clear of the building now, right?"

"Yes," I said, doing a quick survey of the crowd. Everyone seemed accounted for.

"Then let's do this."

We made our way back to the front of the crowd, Zashil and Fred asking everyone to step back even more, to give me plenty of space.

Fred brought out his phone and swiped it, searching for the blueprints. There was that message again. This time I caught the name of the sender. K.W. That was entirely unhelpful. Not that it mattered to me anyway.

"Here we are," he said, holding the phone out in front of me. "Now, chin up. Fly right. I'm sure even a skinny little thing like you can get this done."

Was that supposed to be a compliment of some sort? I bit down a rising tide of annoyance.

"You can do this, Dahlia," said Zashil, standing on my other side.

Taking a deep breath, I reached both hands out before me and opened my mouth to speak.

"You sure that's *all* you need to do? Wave your hands around a bit? Doesn't seem like you're doing much, sweetheart," said Fred.

I tried not to picture myself strangling him and focused on the spell.

"YTILAER A SNGISED ESEHT EKAM," I said, channeling every bit of magical energy I could summon, focusing it through the tip of my hat and down through my arms out of my hands. "STNIR-PEULB ESEHT TIF OT GNIDLIUB DLO SIHT MROFSNART!"

It was possibly the longest spell I'd ever spoken, my brain straining to capture the words and find a way to pronounce them backward.

My arms ached with the flow of energy, shaking, but I kept them steady. The magic poured from my hands like a torrent of wind, the crowd behind me letting out a little gasp as the bowling alley stretched and groaned with the clink of glass, the thunk of lumber, the tap, tap, tapping of pure force on nails.

My brow was damp a minute later, the flimsy shawl I'd used to buffet against the cold now like a wool blanket on a hot, summer day.

The outside façade was the last thing to transform, the simple fixing of the window, the coat of paint on the door, the sign overhead warping into new words almost too much for me to handle.

"Dahlia, you're almost finished!" said Zashil.

"Hang in there, hotcakes!" Fred was really messing with my concentration. But I put all of myself into it, seeing the enchantment through to the end.

Letting out a cry, I collapsed to my knees, just as the world went quiet around me.

Staring at the hard concrete below me, I didn't have a chance to see if it was all done.

Fred let out a riotous laugh. "She did it!" I witnessed his shiny brown shoes scuffle past me as the door opened feet in front of me. "She actually did it!" he repeated from inside.

Everyone in the crowd let out a joyful cry.

"Dahlia." Zashil was at my side, soon followed by Faine and Cable, all three pulling together to bring me up to wobbly legs. Broomie moved in swiftly behind me, as if to catch me should I fall again.

"Thank you," Zashil whispered. "You're amazing."

Chapter Eight

I took in the sight of my enchantment. It looked… fine. *Spooky Escape Rooms* was emblazoned over the door, the finest detail like the spiderwebs across the glass window, all in place.

Some of the crowd was migrating through the open door, but I got a good look. It was a stylish lobby, complete with a computer at a counter and soft, red plush benches lined up by the wall and the window. My enchantment had even captured the stylish logo on the wall behind the counter at which Fred now stood.

My friends guided me inside, Zashil crying out for those in front of us to make way.

They parted like the tall grass in a meadow on a windy day, letting me be guided to one of the benches. Cable and Faine sat on either side of me, Broomie curling up in my lap, and Zashil joined his parents and husband to confer with Fred near the counter. Their faces were positively alight as they gazed around and took in the place. Fred and Zashil looked under the counter and produced a set of keys, unlocking a door in the corner and disappearing into the back.

Though the doors were likely among the material delivered, complete with locks attached, my enchantment had even put the keys in an easily accessible place.

I stared at my hands, which were still trembling.

"I can't believe you managed all this," said Faine softly, though I still heard her from amidst the buzzing of the crowd continuing to spill in. With the former bowling alley now divvied up into the single escape room and the employees-only area, the lobby was the only easily accessible place—and it could hardly hold this number of people.

Cable laid a hand on my shoulder, softly, hesitatingly. "Are you all right?" he asked. "You look a bit pale."

I removed my hat and wiped my brow with my forearm, the cold iciness of my stone scales suddenly quite welcome. "I'm a bit tired." My voice cracked.

"Is there some water around here?" Faine wondered, gazing around.

But before she could ask anyone, the door to the back slammed open, knocking against the wall, and Fred popped out of it, his hands to each side like a circus ringleader. He surveyed the crowd like a king before a feast, and then his gaze fell on me. "By golly, Dahlia, you did it." Before I could blink, he was across the room, had gripped my face by both cheeks, and planted a sloppy kiss on my damp forehead.

Cable startled *for* me, his hand slipping from one shoulder across to the other and pulling me against his chest.

My heart thundered in my ears. His coat felt so soft and fuzzy against my cheek. I almost didn't want to sit up again.

Fred didn't seem bothered by any of it as he spun on his heel and addressed the crowd. "Distinguished people of Luna Lane, please, please, I appreciate your interest, but we do have crowd control to worry about." His eye fell on Sherriff Roan just outside the door, who nodded.

"I was just about to say. Max capacity twenty people in this lobby, I'd venture. Come on out, everyone."

The murmuring crowd erupted into a collective groan and filed out. I sat up straighter, slowly, my head fuzzy. My nose practically grazed Cable's as I pulled back, and we stared at one another, not saying a word.

If I weren't so exhausted, I could figure out what to say—what had just happened.

"Thank you," was all I managed. He'd reacted when Fred had manhandled me before I'd even thought to.

Cable's brow furrowed, but as he opened his lips, he was drowned out by Fred's little yelp of delight. "They're all going to be customers," he said. "And there's plenty of room back there. We can expand to add a second room in a matter of weeks." He spun on his heel. "If our lovely witch would be willing to help speed that along as well. From the looks of it, everyone in town might be done with the first room by then."

I nodded lazily, the words not fully reaching my brain.

"Let's wait and see how this enchantment affected her," said Cable, standing. He was just slightly taller than Fred and managed to grow intimidating, with the way he straightened his back and shifted his weight as if planting himself between me and a force of nature.

"Yes, yes, of course," said Fred, waving a hand at me. "I have other locations to visit regardless. Zashil will tell me how the first few weeks of operation go and I'll swing back for the expansion."

Oh, goody. I could hardly wait for his return.

Zashil was speaking to his parents and got Fred's attention. They spoke in hushed tones, and Faine stood. "Let me run down to the café. Get you something to drink and eat." She smiled. "Amazing work, Dahlia. I knew you had it in you."

I laughed. *Had* she known, though? Had anyone? Had *I*?

"Thank you," I said as she slipped out the door and into the crowd.

"Here," said Cable, handing the bag of oatcakes back to me. He ran a hand over the back of his head. "Though that might just make you more thirsty—"

Ripping open the bag, I popped an oatcake into my mouth. A sense of satisfaction spread over me.

Cable smiled.

Fred stepped toward the open doorway. "Okay, Zashil has informed me that people like his elderly parents here don't know how an escape room even works, is that right?"

Goldie—hardly *elderly*—shifted in place uncomfortably. "Zashil tried to explain it to us."

"No, no, no, Mrs. Mahajan, you must not be ashamed," said Fred. "We are proud to be the first —and only, I hope—escape room in Luna Lane." He clapped his hands together at the crowd, his gaze resting hungrily on Spindra closest to him.

"It's simple, really, and your gamemaster will go over it before you play." Fred was soaking up the attention, and each eye in the crowd that I could see seemed riveted by him. "But the basics are: You're locked in a room for sixty minutes—"

Mayor Abdel raised his hand, his wrappings making him stand out.

"Yes, mayor?" Fred gripped his hands together in front of him, his jaw clenching just slightly at the interruption.

"That doesn't seem safe," said the mayor. "What if a fire—"

"Players are perfectly free to abort the game should an emergency arise," said Fred. "Our gamemaster will be watching through the surveillance cameras overhead, and the moment someone needs to use the restroom or take a phone call or just feels overwhelmed and needs some fresh air, we promise to unlock you and stop the game. No refunds, though, you understand." He added that last part quickly.

Broomie shook her bristles on my lap and stretched out across the rest of the bench in the area Faine had vacated. A beam of sunlight filtered in through the fake spiderwebs in the window behind us, projecting a warped, spooky pattern on the bench and floor at our feet.

"I wonder why it has to *actually* be locked, then," said Cable under his breath. I looked up at him and he shrugged, crossing his arms. "Players can just pretend, can't they?"

Fred swiveled toward Cable, tightlipped, but didn't respond to him, turning back to the crowd. "Inside the themed room is a series of puzzles," he continued. "Each puzzle unlocks a clue you'll need to solve something else. In our first themed room"— he gestured to a door behind Goldie and Arjun —"players start in a set of jail cells in the basement of a top-secret prison, the players split into three groups."

Jamie lifted his hand and spoke before being called upon. "What if there aren't three players?"

"Good question." Fred started pacing, his hands clasped behind his back. "We have a three-player minimum for this specific room. Though other designs in the Spooky Escape Rooms franchise can be done with a minimum of two—but let me tell you, the more, the merrier. The better your chances of solving the room. Remember, there's a time limit."

"How many maximum can play?" asked Arjun.

"Nine in this particular room." Fred leaned against the door leading to the secret prison design. "We have some rooms that take up to twelve. And, during busy seasons, we may have to pair you with strangers who want to play if you don't book the entire maximum capacity."

That would make for a strange introduction to new people. Thank goodness there were no strangers in Luna Lane. By the time their marketing drove in out-of-towners, it seemed like all of the town's citizens would have leaped at a chance to play.

Fred wasn't finished. "Get all three groups out of each jail cell, solve the rest of the puzzles, and free yourselves from the prison entirely. Then you win!"

"What do you win?" asked Chione.

"Satisfaction, my dear." Fred beamed and scrambled to the counter. He pulled out a black T-shirt with the logo for the escape room emblazoned across it. "A discount off any of our fine merchandise," he continued. "And the team that holds the record for best time each month gets a free button!" He whipped out a bag of cheap, plastic buttons from behind the counter.

Roan chuckled and moved through the crowd, probably back to his station.

"It's all about the *experience*, my dear miss," said Fred, moving closer to the door. He was taking a good look at Chione now—stern and all business, but beautiful nonetheless—and I'd had just about enough of this playboy and his unwarranted confidence.

"Let's head to the café," I said to Cable, nudging Broomie to wake her up. Cable took my arm before I even realized it, helping me to my feet. He grabbed the bag with the last few oatcakes from me and tucked it in his coat pocket, then looped his arm through mine once I'd stood straighter. My face flushed as Broomie stretched and glided into my other hand.

"When are you open?" Jamie asked eagerly. His hand had shot over his head, but again, he hadn't even bothered to wait for anyone to call on him.

Fred chortled. "Always with the most pertinent questions, my fine young man." He turned to Zashil behind him. "Well, we need to do a few practice runs with the staff—and Zash's family has kindly volunteered to do those test runs with us while we make sure there are no kinks." He seemed to notice me halfway to the door at that point and turned to me. "Not that we expect them to be any fault of yours, mind you, but we just need to have the gamemasters familiar with the puzzles and the timing."

I wasn't going to suppose anything that went wrong with the games was my fault, but now I had that thought rolling through my head.

Oh, well. I couldn't expect to get things perfect the first time I'd tried such a monumental enchantment.

Cable exchanged a look with me, his eyes rolling, as if to dismiss what Fred had said entirely.

There were murmurs from the crowd.

"You'll all know the moment we open! But you, young man." He gestured toward Jamie.

Jamie looked behind him, then pointed to himself, mouthing, "Me?"

"Yes, you, of course," answered Fred to the unasked question. "You've shown such initiative and asked about joining the team. Why don't you do the trial run with us? Think of it as your job interview."

Jamie positively beamed, slipping past Chione and Spindra to get inside just as Cable, Broomie, and I exited.

A few other hands shot up in the crowd and Fred laughed as he moved to shut the door behind us. "Thank you, thank you for your interest. You will all have a turn, I swear to you. But please give us a chance to do a few run-throughs."

The door shut behind us and the crowd began to disperse, everyone breaking into smaller groups walking off every which way. Few people drove around town in Luna Lane. Other than Chione, who chauffeured her great-great-etcetera grandfather around in a shiny red Ferrari. She held the passenger's side door open to him as we passed by on the sidewalk.

"Need a lift?" Mayor Abdel asked.

"Thank you. I'm still a bit tired. That would be helpful," I said, though Broomie bristled in my hand. She wanted to take me, I was sure, but Cable was here—still holding me by the arm—and he was nervous about flying on her again. "It's all right." I hushed her. She shook at the sight of the car and wormed her way out of my hand, shaking her bristles before speeding away without me.

"She doesn't like me," Cable said as Chione opened the back door for us and we both thanked her.

"She doesn't like cars," I corrected. She *loved* Cable. Mostly, she loved teasing him. "She'll shake it off, meet me up back home. It's about time for her nap anyway."

Chione shut the door after we'd climbed in and then walked around the car to get behind the steering wheel.

"Where to?" Abdel asked.

"The café," I said. "You might see Faine along the way. She went back to get me some water."

"You'd think they would have thought of that," said Chione wryly. She adjusted the rearview mirror and locked her dark eyes on mine. She looked so much better now that she'd healed from her vampire venom addiction. The thought of venom made me shudder, remembering Draven's revelation. "Making you do all that work and not bothering to offer you something to refresh yourself," she explained.

"You think they'd let her get first crack at the game," Abdel added.

"Oh, I don't mind that," I said.

"She wants to wait until Games Club can do it together," Cable added.

I did? So I did, apparently. There was no escaping the escape room at this point.

"Yeah," I said. "Best let them get the kinks out or whatever."

"Draven's not going to like Jamie working there," said Abdel after a few minutes of silence. We took a turn at a leisurely pace.

"Surely, he can still work at the pub," said Chione, licking her lips. "How many hours can you put in at an escape room?"

"Eight to ten hours a day, from the way Fred and Zashil pitched it to me," said Mayor Abdel. We pulled up to the café already. The walk wouldn't have been so bad, really, except I felt so tired.

The door opened with a jingle and Faine stepped out, a plastic drink cup and a baggie in her hand.

"Oh, we caught her just in time. Faine!" Cable opened the back door to the car. "Thanks for the ride," he said to Chione, slipping out of the car and swiftly moving to help Faine with what she was carrying.

I started sliding out after him, but Abdel stopped me, his wrappings rougher than I'd expected as his hand slammed over mine atop the seat.

"Do you think we're making a mistake?" he asked me.

Chione shifted in her seat, seemingly eager for my answer, too.

The door to the café jingled and Cable and Faine headed inside, probably assuming I'd be right behind them.

"Mistake?" I posited back.

Mayor Abdel let go of my hand and slunk into his seat. "This... escape room. Opening up Luna Lane to so much outside business."

I pinched my lips together. "Well, I do think Fred was overselling it. How many people could it possibly bring in? Especially on weekdays?"

"Maybe." Abdel nodded and seemed lost in thought. "I just didn't have the heart to send Zashil away. The Mahajans are ours. Our humans."

Chione put a hand on his shoulder and I studied them. Did the town hall have doubts, too, then?

"Fred isn't going to stay," I said. "So there's that…"

"He might if Spindra tempts him," said Chione sharply.

"You saw that, too?" asked Abdel.

I snorted. "You'd have to be willfully ignorant not to notice her sinking her hooks into him." I frowned. "But she swore. No killing humans as long as she lives in Luna Lane. It's not even like she *needs* to hurt a human like the vampires do."

"It's just… in her nature," said Chione.

"And we've seen how well our paranormal citizens stick to their promises not to kill anyone in Luna Lane." Abdel frowned, his pouting lips especially hard to ignore amidst the wrappings over most of his face.

So that was what this was about. Regret over not noticing what Ravana had been doing right under his nose for decades.

Shaky confidence that maybe he was making a mistake.

"We'll be okay," I said, patting the back of his chair. "Spindra knows better. She's probably just having some fun—and frankly, that blowhard deserves any bit of *fun* she might offer him. And as for the out-of-towners, it'll probably be confined to the weekend, and we'll all be careful around them. Just a couple of days a week, just a small group or two."

"Don't suppose you could work a memory wipe

enchantment if need be?" Abdel asked, but it was more like he already knew the answer.

"No," I said grimly. I'd never attempted to manipulate a living being that way. Healing physical injuries was hard enough. And besides, memory wipes—that reeked of dark magic. I wouldn't attempt anything my mom never had and that Eithne *had*.

"It'll be okay," I repeated, as much to myself as to him. I did feel better knowing I wasn't the only one with reservations. Bit late to take them too seriously, though.

"Say, have you done your good deed for the day?" Mayor Abdel asked as I got my feet on the sidewalk. "We could use your help at town hall this afternoon."

"Oh, right." I patted my left arm. Despite the massive favor I'd just done someone, it wouldn't count. My fuzzy mind was making me forget. "Thank you. I'll be there. Just need to recharge with some lunch." I gestured at the café behind me. *And pray I feel less wiped after I'm off my feet a bit.*

I was a mix of emotions, exhilarated at having completed such a task, maybe even a bit piggish at the thought that so many people had cautioned me against it, assuming I'd fail. But also weary to my very bones, making me think perhaps they'd been right. It'd been too much.

And Fred wanted me to make them another

room in a few weeks? Why didn't he just ask me to redesign the whole town while he was at it?

"Dahlia! Dahlia! Thank goodness I found you!"

We all turned, Mayor Abdel, Chione, and I, to face the source of the shrieking, harrowing voice as it approached.

Javier, not known for losing his composure, bolted down the block as fast as his legs could take him. He skidded to a stop beside me, clutching at a stich in his muscled side. He must have powered even beyond his bodybuilder limits.

"There's been an accident," he said, his face growing sickly. "At the escape room. Jamie is hurt. And Fred is dead."

Chapter Nine

*M*y knees buckled and collapsed to the ground, the hard concrete scuffing against my rear end.

Hurt? Dead? *Dead?*

Mayor Abdel let out an eerie groan that snapped me back into the moment over the sound of my rapid heartbeat.

Javier was crouching beside me, tugging at my arm. "Zashil and Arjun went to find Doctor Day," he said. "But they said you were basically the local hospital—you could heal the injuries the doctor can't handle."

My mouth bobbed open and closed like a fish's.

"Come on!" said Javier, yanking at me. "Please! We could lose Jamie, too!"

That was like a cold splash of water across the face.

"In the car!" shouted Chione.

That was right. Broomie was nowhere to be found. Oh, if only I hadn't insulted her with the car ride to begin with.

If only I... Oh, goodness. What had I done?

The door to the café burst open, the cheery jingle of the bell overhead like an anvil pounding against my weary brain.

"What's happened?" asked Cable. Faine held the door open behind me, her expression tight as she took in the scene.

Somehow, I'd gotten to my feet, and Cable moved in to steady me.

As comforting as his presence might have proven right now, I had no time for it.

I hopped back into the car. "Drive!" I shouted at Chione, and we took off, leaving Javier behind to explain everything.

Chione shifted the Ferrari into gear and slammed her foot on the accelerator, not bothering to check for any other traffic as she pulled us into a screeching U-turn and back down the way we'd just traveled.

None of us spoke as Chione took us back in half the time. If they were anything like me, the thumping of their hearts, the ringing in their heads would have made it impossible to converse regardless.

Mayor Abdel clutched at where his heart would be—I'd forgotten, he was a mummy, he no longer had one—and moaned, the sound from between his lips almost inhuman.

"Breathe, Grandfather," said Chione as she took a sharp turn. "I know you don't have to, but the memory steadies you. Deep breath in, deep breath out."

Abdel did as she instructed, and his ghastly sound faded just as we pulled up in front of Spooky Escape Rooms again. Barreling out of the car, I bolted inside the storefront, shoving open the door. "I'm here!" I shouted, my feet lighter than they ought to have been.

"In here!" cried a muffled voice I recognized as Goldie's. The door to the prison escape room was propped open, a groan almost as inhuman as Abdel's echoing out from the darkness.

"Where's the light?" I screeched as I stepped inside, but there was no switch behind me.

"WOLG," I said to my fingers, and they practically sparked, flickering, but eventually shone with light.

Uh-oh. That didn't bode well for healing. I was reminded awfully of the time I'd lost my powers thanks to the para-paranormal.

The very same substance Ravana had used on me in this former bowling alley, the last remnants of it then skittering down an empty lane.

The thought that I'd never recovered it made several choice curse words shoot out from my lips.

But no. I wouldn't have been able to have built

this place if it were so close by, if it were enough to cause an issue. The flask had to have been empty. I could do this. I was just running on empty after an enchantment of this caliber.

"Hurry!" cried Goldie, and I followed the sound of her voice to the side of the leftmost jail cell. The cell door was open, a safe on the floor between that and the second cell door. Something hit me from within like an ice cube running down my back, but I ignored it to press on to where Goldie called to me from.

Jamie groaned. He was on his stomach, one leg behind him growing out of the wall, a pool of blood beside him. Far, far too much blood for one person.

"His leg is trapped!" said Goldie, and I realized that there was something in the wall—a hidden door, no bigger than a crawl space in the wall, and it was open just enough to allow for Jamie's leg to be caught under it.

"Zashil got all the doors to open from wherever he was watching us in the back," said Goldie. "But this trap door got stuck!"

"NEPO!" With shaking arms, I pointed at the trap door. It strained my muscles, and it seemed to be taking longer than it ought to have, but eventually, the enchantment took, slowly grinding upward, the sound of gears turning so exaggeratedly harsh, I had to assume it was an intentional sound effect of the experience.

Jamie gasped and grabbed his battered leg with

both arms, yanking it out of the way with a wild cry.

I hoped he wasn't making anything worse with his injury, but I supposed if I were him, I wouldn't want to be anywhere near that trap door anymore, either.

Down the tunnel, no longer than two people stacked on top of one another, was a dim shaft of light from the fake jail cell, leaking around a crumpled form.

"Dahlia!" said Goldie, bringing me back to the moment.

I focused on Jamie. "LAEH." My voice was shaky, the magic energy coming from my fingers more like a tepid breeze than the gust of wind I was hoping for. "GEL SIHT LAEH!"

I hadn't been a powerful enough witch before this to heal anyone of a grievous injury perfectly, though I—thankfully—hadn't had much practice. I certainly wasn't powerful enough now.

But it was enough. With a mangled cry, Jamie fell back, passed out, the pain too much—in my panic, I'd forgotten to cast an enchantment to mute his pain.

But the bleeding stopped, the flattened, mangled appearance of his leg stitched together, the skin covering up any holes as the busted leg started seeming whole again.

His pant leg was shredded and damp with the slightest bit of a mushy, avocado-like stain. I pressed my fingers to it and it came back wet, but it was like whatever it had been had scraped away when he'd pulled his leg out. Turning my attention to the injury, I could see the scars dotting here and there across his leg, but the color was already returning to his face, the leg appearing without a bump or dent, aside from the imperfections on the flesh.

It would have to do.

I let out a harsh breath and collapsed on hands and knees.

And with a sickening crunch, the trap door landed shut with a thud beside me.

"Oh no!" Goldie clawed fingers down her cheeks. "Fred... Fred is still trapped in there."

I felt suddenly, overwhelmingly, about to be sick.

Of course, what Goldie might have been unable to really articulate was that Fred's *body* was still under the trap door at the other end. As I sat on the bench seat I'd rested on just a few hours earlier, a blanket from the sheriff's station wrapped around my shoulders and a coffee cup full of water from the café cradled in my hands, I got the full story.

Faine squeezed my side, her arm wrapped around me in a half-embrace for however long we'd been sitting here.

Sheriff Roan let out a sigh and walked away from the group of witnesses he'd been interviewing in the back, the door opened and the lights on bright so we could see them gathered together: Javier, Zashil, Arjun, and Goldie. He'd already gotten Jamie's statement. Jamie was outside taking slow turns around the block in the last light of the setting sun with Doc Day, and I was pleased to see I'd at least managed to heal him well enough for that. She was going to drive him to the county hospital just to be sure. She had a doctor friend there who knew not to question the cases she brought in from Luna Lane, who helped her fudge the few charts they needed to examine. He stopped by the pub from time to time.

Cable wrung his hands beside me. He hadn't voiced what I'd been thinking. No one had.

But I knew everyone else thought it, too.

This was all my fault.

"So…" Roan slipped his fingers through belt loops at his waist. "It looks like they were playing the game. Zashil was the gamemaster in the back, Arjun in the middle cell, Goldie and Javier in the rightmost cell, and Fred and Jamie together in the leftmost cell."

"The one with the trap door and crawl space," said Cable grimly.

"Yes," said Roan. "The other three players were actually out of their cells by then—they explained you had to solve a series of puzzles to do so—and Arjun had cracked the puzzle that had opened the trap door, allowing Fred and Jamie the chance to escape."

"Arjun solved it?" Faine asked.

"From outside the cells," Roan explained. "Zashil assured me that was quite common in these types of games. The players on one side of the jail cells would have to shout out any clues they found in their own cells until everyone put the pieces together. Whoever had access to the puzzle would then have to input the solution everyone came up with together."

"Was there any chance Arjun solved the puzzle wrong?" Cable's eyes flicked to me and I flinched under his gaze, focusing on the coffee cup with water.

"Sure. He did the first few tries. A wrong answer on a puzzle just means the trap door doesn't move, not that it rises up and allows the pair to start to escape before slamming down on them." Roan grimaced. "Sorry. That was insensitive of me." He sighed. "Seems like there was a malfunction in the mechanics. Arjun inputted the correct solution, the trap door opened, Fred sent Jamie out first, and just as Jamie almost cleared it, it came crashing back down. Zashil's run the same game at another location and said that's never happened before, but there are safety measures in place. First, *the gamemaster* actually controls when the gate lifts. He watches to see if the player inputs the puzzle correctly, and when they push the button, it's the gamemaster who flicks on the trap door controls."

"Kind of seems like a cheat," Cable said weakly. "If the puzzles inside the room aren't actually connected to anything."

"It'd be too hard to wire things that way," Roan explained. It seemed as if this were a question he'd posed himself. "It's safer for the gamemaster to have control—and to be able to override it."

"Which he wasn't able to do this time?" I offered unhelpfully.

Roan shook his head. "No. But… there was something else wrong, something they only noticed when it was too late."

"What is that?" I dreaded the answer.

"It's supposed to be two lightweight doors at each end," Roan said. "Well, that's what Zashil remembers—we'd have to get access to the blue-prints to be sure. But that makes sense. Two plywood doors, an empty space between. If the trap door malfunctions, the most anyone would suffer was a little bump on the head."

My stomach roiled. That wasn't the trap door I'd seen at all. Whatever it had been made of, it had stretched from end to end, and plywood wouldn't have been enough to crush Jamie's leg like that, to squish—

I heaved, but nothing was in my stomach. Faine patted my back and Cable sat down on the other side of me.

"The blueprints were on Fred's phone," Cable offered. Why? Maybe he was trying to shift the blame to the design—I hadn't consciously enchanted a tunnel that way. But it was still *I* who'd done it. *I* who'd agreed to this. A proper crew building the thing the proper way would never have installed such a thing, whatever the blueprints said. This wasn't supposed to be a *real* prison.

"It broke along with the rest of him," said Roan quietly. He sighed and scratched his chin. "I have to get the county in on this. I'm sure an autopsy won't show anything we don't already know, but he's an out-of-towner. There's family to notify and such. City boys and girls might want to do a sweep of the scene."

"They'll shut this place down," said Faine, her voice crackling.

They definitely should.

"They'll want to see building codes, talk to the construction workers," added Cable. "How are we going to explain all that?"

Roan frowned. "We have to notify the family."

Zashil appeared behind him, his eyes sunken, his cheeks puffy. "Fred had no family. An ex-wife, divorced some years back. No kids. No parents left, an only child." It seemed an awful lot of detail for a business partner to know, but Fred had loved to hear himself speak. I could see how his life story would have spilled out to Zashil at some point or another.

Roan bristled. He was clearly at war with

himself, trying to figure out the right thing to do. "Well, he has other business partners, other locations, at the very least. We can't just not let people know—"

Mayor Abdel shuffled inside the open door, loosening his tie. He must have stayed outside in his car the whole time. Or at least I hadn't seen him.

"Can it wait?" he asked. "Just a few more days? Until we figure out what went wrong?"

"What went wrong was I messed up this enchantment." My voice cracked, but I pushed through it, growing louder with each word. My fingers felt suddenly weak and the cup slipped from my hands, spilling water all over the floor. A few drops fell to join the puddle from above and I realized I was crying, my tears streaming down my cheeks. "I should have listened to you all, shouldn't have attempted something like this."

Faine was scrambling to pick up the cup, pulling tissues out from her purse to mop up the water. Zashil took her place beside me on the bench. "I asked you to do it. I *pressured* you—"

"It doesn't change the fact that I did it."

Everyone was quiet for a bit, Faine clutching the sodden tissues in her hand.

Outside, a mumbling indicating another gathering crowd drew our attention. Mayor Abdel turned on his heel. "A few days, Roan. We have to figure out our story. We have to protect our own." He offered me a feeble smile and left.

No denying I'd been the culprit. Just… covering up my massive mistake.

I cradled my face with my hands.

Roan let out a deep breath. "Coroner's team is on the way, but I'll pull a few strings again, get them to lose the paperwork for a few days. That's the most I can stretch this." He patted my shoulder. "It was an accident."

"I should have looked at Fred!" I said suddenly, jumping up. "I could save him—"

"There was nothing you could do," said Zashil quietly. "He was gone, Dahlia. His skull…" He stopped himself.

I couldn't mend *that*.

I felt suddenly faint, and Cable swooped in to catch me.

"Your name won't even come up," said Roan. He slid his notepad into his front pocket. "Abdel and I need to figure out how to explain the construction without pinning the blame on anyone else."

"I'll help." Zashil stood. "Look over what records Fred brought with him, see if one of the other partners can send over the blueprints." His chest hitched and there were still tears behind his eyes. "It's the least I can do."

Roan nodded, and he left to talk to Abdel and likely disperse the gathering crowd. Zashil squeezed my hand, then went back to his family still waiting in the back.

I was left in awkward silence with Cable and

Faine. Faine was near the trash can behind the counter. I wished desperately Broomie were nearby so I could fly off and hide, as far away as this wretched curse would take me.

"Where's Milton?" I asked, suddenly aware that with both Cable and Doc Day occupied here, he'd been left alone for quite a while. I didn't even know how long. My head throbbed.

"Grady and the kids are with him at the café," offered Faine.

"The kids…?" What time was it?

Both Faine and Cable seemed to realize what I was thinking at once, their faces growing pale.

"Dahlia, did you do your good deed today? One without magic?"

My gaze flicked out the window behind Cable. The last bit of sunlight was fading behind the horizon.

My left arm grew hot with searing pain. A cry flew past my lips and I collapsed to my knees, sore with bruises from too much falling in one day.

"Dahlia!" cried Faine and Cable, both crouching at my side.

But there was no stopping it.

My curse couldn't forgive me one day—not one single day when I'd already given all of myself I had to give to help others. Not one day in which my own hands had killed someone.

The scale spread and grew over the back of my left hand, melding with the few smaller scales that existed over the wrist to coat nearly the entire back. It was only me flexing my knuckles in panic that the stone would freeze my joints that seemed to hold the scale's growth back, leaving me the ability to flex—stiffly, but there was movement at least.

When it was done, the edges of the stone scale met with red, irritated flesh.

Faine patted my back. "I'm so sorry," she said. "So sorry about everything today." She embraced me on the floor, my tears coming out like thunder now, though I realized with a start that the sky itself was rumbling with the beginnings of a storm. Faine whimpered in my arms. We stayed like that for a long, quiet moment.

With a screech and a pop, a bat flew inside the Spooky Escape Rooms waiting room and revealed itself to be Draven, his pale, lithe form accentuated by the flash of light far off in the distance behind him.

"Dahlia," he said. Broomhilde of all creatures flew in right behind him. "What have you done?" His accusing, sharp, red-rimmed eyes and his heavy sigh were the last straw.

I jumped on Broomhilde and took off into the night without another word to anyone.

Chapter Ten

*B*roomie must have forgiven me for choosing the car over her because we were soaring together now, high over the last few houses that dotted the outskirts of Luna Lane, the cries of my name on the tongues of Faine, Cable, and Draven long behind me, their emotional pleas like nails on a chalkboard in the face of my sins.

I'd been a fool. Didn't they think I knew that by now? What more did they want from me? Was I doomed to rehash it with everyone one by one, searching for a way to undo what I had done?

Whether it was my own lack of skill, the potential if faint presence of the para-paranormal somewhere deep inside the recesses of that building somehow tampering with my work… Even if it had been a flaw in Fred's blueprints, which seemed doubtful… Either way, I should have known better than to do that.

Without directing her anywhere specific, Broomie flew us out to the woods surrounding town, past a few choice locations for potions ingredients, and kept going until we were almost as far as the curse would let me go. There, she settled us by a small lake, landing next to the remnants of a campsite someone had used long ago. Scorched dirt and half-burnt logs made its purpose clear. Stones arranged to face the fire acted as seats for a group of at least five.

There'd be only me and Broomie tonight, though.

I patted her as she took us down, gently nudging me onto the stone seat closest to the water. She understood me, our bond conveying what I'd needed to her. Still, I wished we could communicate in absolute terms. It had almost seemed like she'd come *with* Draven. What had she been up to after we'd parted?

But I supposed if I'd really wanted to know, I could have stayed behind and asked the vampire.

Squeezing my thighs to my chest, I wrapped my arms around my legs and stared at the moonlight dancing over the still waters.

My stomach rumbled and I remembered I'd had nothing but oatcakes to eat all day. At least they'd been somewhat hearty. I wasn't so hungry as to feel faint.

I wasn't sure how long I sat there, thinking, Broomie leaned up against my side. My body ached, the back of my palm itched and felt heavy, like it was weighing down my appendage. But still, I sat silently.

There was no sound alerting me to the figure's approach because without choosing to be corporeal, she wouldn't disturb anything around us.

"Miss Poplar."

Virginia glided out from the direction of Luna Lane, but she'd come a long way.

"I didn't know you went for strolls in the woods," I said, my chin barely leaving my knee as I spoke.

"Not typically, no." She hover-sat on the stone stool beside me, crossing her legs gingerly at the ankle to the side, almost like riding a horse sidesaddle.

I stared at her as the thunder rumbled somewhere off in the distance, the promised rain never showing, at least not where I sat. Without her parasol, without even her hat, Virginia sat in the moonlight and gazed out at the surface.

"You've heard, I take it?" I asked. Unless she was still miffed about me almost forgetting she'd been in the bowling alley before I'd cast my enchantment.

"I have." Her lips were pinched as she stared forward.

"I'm sorry about almost forgetting you," I said, putting my feet back on the ground, my hands clutching my skirt at my knees. "I was just so nervous—"

"Please." She put a hand over mine. It was like an ice pack, just a wisp of breeze at first until she made it become corporeal. "Water under the bridge." Still, she looked forward, the light in her eyes that usually sparkled there gone, as muted as the rest of her. She pulled away.

And then it dawned on me.

"Your house." She'd told me she'd burned to death in her home, which had once been on the very same site of that bowling alley.

"My house?" asked Virginia.

"You died there... In that same place. A different way, sure, but I thought maybe... Another death there had reminded you."

Virginia's eyes widened. "Yes, yes, of course. Of course that bothered me. But I was mostly worried about you." She shifted in her seat to face me entirely. "You didn't kill him, you know."

"Not on purpose." I rubbed the new scale on the back of my hand subconsciously, and Broomie nudged my arm, as if to offer me solace.

"No, I mean... It wasn't your fault. At all. You cannot blame yourself."

"I do, though."

Virginia bit her lip and took my left hand in both of hers. She frowned. "This is new."

I yanked my hand backward, tugging on my

shawl to hide my arm beneath it entirely. "I got more than a little sidetracked today."

"Understandable."

We sat in silence again. I wasn't used to so much quiet around Virginia.

"And you were so excited," I said, for want of something to talk about. It felt worse in the silence when someone was here with me. "About Games Club doing the escape room."

Virginia fluffed her hand on me. "*I* couldn't play that game now."

I understood what she meant. Even if it did manage to stay open, which seemed incredibly unlikely. Zashil had seemed to understand that. His countenance was that of someone who'd not just lost… a friend, if that was what Fred had been to him… but of someone who'd lost all idea of his tomorrows.

Though my options were far more limited than his, I at least understood that feeling. What was left for me? Numbly perform the smallest of tasks day after day after day? Give up on magic entirely?

It'd be so much easier to spend the next few days here and let my entire body turn to stone.

"How'd you find me?" I asked, the question suddenly occurring to me. How did she ever find anyone? She always appeared at random times, in random places. But those were all in town at least. I'd never met her here in the woods.

"I was looking for you," she said simply. "I

spotted you and followed you, though I can't match Broomhilde's speed."

Broomie cooed beside me, nudging at Virginia for her compliment. Virginia didn't solidify, though, so my broom brushed right through.

Like a cat, she had a habit of pretending she'd "meant to do that" when things didn't go her way. Where a cat might have licked herself casually, she just floated on through, settling in a lazy circle in the brush some distance away and flicking her brush back like a woman with long hair.

I watched her, and when she popped up, a peculiar thing hung from the top of her brush.

"What's that?" I asked, getting off the stone seat and edging closer to her. Virginia floated with me.

A half-shattered flask hung upside down off Broomie's bristles, coated in dirt and dust but so like the ones I used myself.

"Broomie, hold still." I reached forward to gently extricate the flask from her, being careful not to cut myself on the broken glass. "What…?" I looked around us. Beneath the tall grass, between the weeds, were the decaying remnants of a life left behind.

"What happened here?" asked Virginia. "What's that?"

I bent down to inspect a plank, chipped and warped with bits of grass and wildflowers poking out through what had once been knots in the wood. "Flooring, I think."

Virginia floated around, and I observed her moving in a fairly defined large square. "You're right. I think there was a cabin here once. Long ago, by the looks of it."

Broomie used her bristles to brush aside some moss on the plank in front of me.

What I saw there made sense, given the partial flask in my hand. But it made my blood run cold regardless.

Runes.

"This was a witch's home. Eithne." I shot to my feet. "You must have known she lived here."

Virginia bristled, laying her fingertips across her breast. "I don't know what you mean."

"You've been a ghost for over a hundred years! You've been in town long enough to know Eithne lived here, in the woods, before my mom came."

Virginia floated closer, making an effort to put one delicate boot-covered foot on the ground. "Miss Poplar, before you get your undergarments in a bunch, you calm yourself down."

I realized then that I'd been squeezing the broken flask in my palm. I dropped it, wincing at the trickle of blood I'd drawn.

"LAEH," I said softly to it. It was such a small cut, the enchantment worked quickly, but I was so spent, the edges of my vision went black.

Plopping down on the ground, I traced the star-shaped rune with my fingertips.

"That's better." Virginia cleared her throat.

"Now, I told you, I hardly ever make my way to these woods. *I* didn't know this house was here, and that is the honest truth." Her lips pinched.

"But you knew Eithne was out here somewhere?" I gestured around me. If I'd just asked Draven where she'd lived precisely, I could have found this place a month ago. But what good would it have done? There didn't seem to be a forgotten book left behind with all the answers about curses and how to combat them. There wasn't even a drop of potion left somewhere in a flask.

"I am aware of the witch who cursed you and ended your mother," said Virginia, her button nose turned up in the air. "May I ask what my awareness matters to you?"

Why did it matter? The immortal—or long-existing, anyway, in Virginia's case—citizens of Luna Lane had once lived side by side in this sleepy little town with Eithne Allaway, a witch who never did anything for anyone if she didn't deprive some benefit from it—even if it was just amusement. I couldn't blame them for that. I hadn't existed, and they hadn't seemed aware of the more harmful activities she'd participated in.

But still, somehow... I just felt betrayed.

Not even my mother—

Mom. Eithne had claimed she'd *helped* Mom move to Luna Lane. Unless she'd managed a mind wipe on her afterward, which I supposed was possible, or had pulled the strings without Mom ever really knowing, Mom would have known about Eithne in Luna Lane.

Eithne had even—laughably—suggested they'd once been friends.

And I'd yet to ask Mom about it. Life had been too peaceful since we'd sent Ravana away, and the times I could call Mom to this realm were limited, dwindling in duration with each occasion I summoned her.

But I had more than just burning curiosity to talk to her about. She'd know where I'd gone wrong in my enchantment—even if it was just to confirm I never should have agreed to rush through something I hadn't understood.

No answer could make me feel better, but at least, if I knew it had been some mistake with my magic, I could stop myself from repeating it.

I leaped to my feet. "I have to speak with my mother."

"Your mother?" Virginia frowned. "Is that such a good idea?"

Broomie was already in place between my legs, and I gripped on to her handle, ready to launch. "I know her time returning here is limited, but there're a few things I absolutely must know. Do me a favor? Poke around here and if you find anything—no matter how insignificant—let me know."

Virginia put both hands on her hips. "Miss Poplar, I am certainly not your landscaper! Do I look dressed for this kind of work?" She held up her lacy gloves.

But I was already launching upward, the sky letting out one last rumble in the distance. If Virginia didn't feel like examining the house, I knew where it was now, and I could go back.

But first… First, I needed to speak to the only person I could trust to provide me with answers.

Chapter Eleven

I'd ingested every bit of power-boosting potion I had left and had swallowed down a few crackers I'd found in my cupboard for good measure. I could hardly sleep, rest, and wait now that the idea was so entrenched in my head.

"RALPOP NOMANNIC, EMOC!" I shouted at the rune circle before me. The carved symbols glowed and in the midst of the circle, a shaky, translucent pile of yellow poplar blossoms and a bundle of cinnamon sticks was shimmering into existence. *Bananaberries*. I was too tired for this. "REHTOM YM, EMOC!" I shouted, putting my all into it.

The blossoms and cinnamon vanished, replaced instead by the faded afterimage of the witch who'd been my mother.

"Mom!" I cried out, falling to my sore and wobbly knees.

"Dahlia?" Mom's youthful face screwed up in consternation as she glided on her spectral broom to the very edge of the rune circle. It was as far as she could go, trapped in a microcosmic echo of my own situation.

I reached a hand out to her, but of course, her fingers felt like air when they brushed mine.

Her face was so similar to mine, almost a reflection of my own, though there were fine wrinkles around the lips, at the corners of the eyes. A single silver streak ran through her fiery-orange hair, pulled back behind her head.

"You look exhausted." Mom zeroed in on the scale on the back of my hand and gasped. "Another scale? *Dahlia!*"

"I know, please." My throat was dry. "I've only grown two since I saw you last." I guiltily covered up the other large one at the top of my arm. "I've been careful, really—but I have other problems."

Mom's lips pursed in that particular way she had, like she was wary of letting some misbehavior go but willing to let it slip at the prospect of something more important to focus on. "Leana passed," she said, when I wasn't immediately forthcoming. She smiled. "We were so happy to find one another. She told me you freed her."

Well, that was good news. Knowing Mom and the woman I'd viewed like a grandmother had moved on—that they were together.

But even good news had so little impact on my wretched mood.

"Me and half the town," I said. An exaggeration, but I definitely hadn't done it alone.

Mom gripped Broomhannah, her partnered broom who had passed beyond to the other realm alongside her, petting her soothingly. Broomhilde chirruped from the edge of the circle, simultaneously excited and sad to see her friend.

"Mom, I messed up." The words came out like hiccups.

Mom's smile vanished. "What happened?"

I told her about the escape room enchantment, about Fred's death. I didn't know how much time we had together, so I kept it as straight to the point as possible.

Mom listened intently, letting me pour it all out.

I hiccupped at the end of it, feeling more like a five-year-old child than a thirty-year-old woman.

Off in my bedroom, Mom's old cuckoo clock struck midnight.

"Dahlia, you need to rest," said Mom softly.

"I will, but not until I know."

"Know what?" Mom asked. "From what you told me, the problem has to have lain with the blueprints. You didn't design anything. From the words you uttered, your magic wouldn't have been capable of twisting the blueprints. Not so specifically, certainly."

"But I—"

"Did you know exactly what you were designing?" she asked. I opened my mouth to explain I knew it was an escape room lobby, office, and prison-themed puzzle room, but she continued. "Down to every lock, every puzzle, the trap door?"

"No," I admitted. "I didn't think I could focus on that much detail. Fred told me he'd used the blueprints at other locations before, so I trusted his designs to put all those little details together." I hiccupped again and Broomie brushed her bristles against my cheek, which stung but felt so sweet and comforting.

Mom nodded. "While I don't recommend you attempt such big enchantments without working your way up to them, it wasn't your fault. Someone must have tampered with the blueprints—or changed the design after the spell was cast."

I laughed. "Who else could? It was less than an hour after I finished that Fred died—"

I went quiet. I knew exactly who could. No construction worker, no human, no mummy, or even vampire.

But another witch could.

Mom wrinkled her brow.

I quickly spilled to her about my confrontation last month with Eithne, the silver-haired witch who'd made her first appearance in Luna Lane since that night ten years ago when I'd come home to find her standing over Mom's body.

"But what would she have to gain from this

man's death?" Mom proposed. She didn't seem at all surprised by Eithne's return.

The tips of her fingers and her slippers were fading. We were running out of time. I cursed under my breath.

"Mom, Eithne told me you and she were once friends! That she helped you move to Luna Lane."

Mom leaned back, her bottom sliding effortlessly atop Broomhannah. Even Broomhannah's bristles were fading now. "We were," she said, her eyes darting to the circle below her.

"*What?*" I clutched the fabric of my dress. "That's not true. It can't be."

"It was the truth," Mom said simply. Her feet and hands were harder to see now. "There's a lot you don't know about my life before you were born—"

"Because you never told me anything!" I jumped up to my feet, startling Broomie to the point where she skidded across the room.

Mom's eyes grew dull, her features downturned. "I'm sorry," she said simply.

She was half-faded now.

"Wait!" I cried. "Mom, please! Don't go!"

"Dahlia, it was always your blood," Mom said. "I should have told you. The k—"

But she was gone.

I'd gotten some possible answers. I had so many more questions.

And I didn't like a single answer I had.

What was always my blood? What had she been about to tell me?

Part of me wanted to summon her again, right this very instant, but I knew from past experience that I had to wait a while between summons. And she had limited possible visits left before her pathway here from the realm beyond shut forever.

And then there was the fact that I was so weak, I was about to pass out.

No, I had to wait. And plan what I would ask, what I would get her to say.

Right now, Eithne was out there—probably having caused Fred's death. But why?

There was a knock on the door. Despite the hour, I knew my friends were worried about me. I couldn't exactly ignore it.

Shuffling to the door, I tugged my shawl tighter around me. Turning the door handle, I started my apology. "I'm sorry for worrying—"

The sight of Draven, alone, cut it short.

His lips pursed, he pointed above him, beyond my covered porch to the sky. "It's nearing the full moon."

Right. Faine got more dog-like at night the closer the full moon came, and though we worried the exposure to para-paranormal last full moon might have impacted the local werewolves' cycle, we couldn't be sure.

"Cable…?" I asked, though I'd hardly have expected Draven to acquiesce to doing anything with the visiting professor alone.

"He had to take his uncle home," said Draven simply. "I assured him you were just in one of your moods. It's late for humans. Well, most of them."

"*Moods?*" I hadn't missed that.

The vampire sighed and flicked a lock of his long, blond hair over his shoulder. "May I come in?"

I wanted to slam the door in his face.

He turned on his heel. "Right. Then I'll be seeing you around. If you stop avoiding me." I'd forgotten he'd claimed vampires could *sense* intent about whether or not they were welcome in a home.

"Fine," I said, relenting, letting the tightness grasping my chest loosen. "Come in."

Draven tucked his hands in his pants pockets and shuffled inside. I shut the door and then stepped back. I had about one tiny spark of energy keeping me standing, so this had better be quick, whatever it was he wanted from me.

"I apologize," he said.

That was the last thing I'd expected.

Broomie's little snores from the couch permeated the air between us.

"For what?" I asked. Where to begin?

"For snapping at you like that back at the escape room. I awoke from my coffin at sunset to find

Broomhilde spinning around like the world was on fire, and I thought the worst."

"Broomie was in *your* basement?" They'd arrived at the escape room at the same time, but I'd never have imagined she'd gone to fetch him. I stared at the sleeping broom. Though we could convey feelings to one another, I wished more than ever she could speak to me, too.

"She was. Qarinah ran out to see if we could discover what was the matter while I tried to calm her. We ran into Spindra almost straight away."

"Spindra?" That spiderwoman had certainly been out and about a lot today. She usually preferred to keep to her tailor's shop, to the dark corners and sticky webs she wove while doing her work. Had Fred interested her that much?

The thought of the dead man made my knees buckle, and I leaned back against the couch.

Draven moved in to impede my fall but stopped himself when he found the couch had been enough to support me.

"Did Spindra tell you, then?" I asked.

"She did. Half the town knew already by then, I suppose." He grunted. "I always wake up the last to know the town's news."

"Fortunately, there usually isn't much of it."

Draven planted his hands on his hips and nodded. "Though there has been as of late."

I swallowed, a sudden thought occurring to me.

Eithne may have had a role, but as for her motivations… "Did Spindra seem different at all?"

"Different?"

It was just a theory, a poor one at that. If a spiderwoman wanted to eat a man, she had plenty of methods of her own to seduce and devour him. But who else had shown such a reciprocated interest in the chatterbox? I'd no doubt her affections hadn't run deep, but she'd seized on him like a tasty snack.

"Dahlia, if you don't tell me what you're thinking, I can't help you," said Draven. I realized I'd gone quiet.

Yes, help *me*. Somehow, it was up to me to uncover the truth of what had happened in our little Luna Lane.

And I had to know. Both because I'd played an unintentional role in Fred's demise—no matter what, he wouldn't have died today if I hadn't built his escape room so quickly—and because Eithne simply could not run amuck in our town.

"I'm just covering my bases." I quickly explained Spindra's behavior around the man, as well as my visit with my mother. Only I left the bit about the blood out of it. Somehow, discussing blood with the one vampire who'd ever tasted mine just sent an uncomfortable shiver up my spine. One problem at a time. "I found the remains of Eithne's cabin in the woods," I finished. "It was an accident, but I went off to be alone and there it was."

Draven listened intently to everything I had to

say. "I could have shown you where it was," he said, focusing on the latest discovery. "If you'd asked earlier."

I swallowed. "So that was where you went to offer her a kiss?"

He smiled slightly. "Does that bother you? The kiss part?"

"You wish," I said, crossing my arms across my chest. We were getting entirely off-track. "So... Spindra. Do you think I should talk to her?"

He shrugged. "You can, if only to put your mind at ease. But do you really think a paranormal resident of Luna Lane would break the rule that—" He cut himself short. Yes, a paranormal resident would kill despite Mayor Abdel's edict that there would be no murders in his town. Draven's own sire had been perpetuating murders for decades under our very noses.

"She did seem upset," he said simply. "More emotion I'd ever seen from her in all the years I've known her. Though that's not to say she was broken up about it or anything."

"What do you mean?"

His shoulder bobbed slightly. "Her voice cracked."

"Her *voice cracked*?"

"Just once, at the mention of Fred's... accident. Have you ever known her to speak of anything in any manner other than cool and composed?"

"And seductive?" I added. "No, I suppose not."

But if that really was the extent of her unexpected behavior, I had to hand it to Draven for his keen observation skills. I didn't think I could manage the same.

"But that wasn't all I came to tell you," Draven said simply. "I investigated the accident site after everyone left. I found… more of it."

"More of what?"

"The red ectoplasm. Para-paranormal."

My stomach roiled. "You're sure it wasn't blood?"

Draven scoffed and tapped his nose. "I *know* blood. And I'd recognize this foul stuff after the events of last month."

"I'd forgotten," I said, my voice quavering, "but a small amount in a flask jettisoned down a lane during the skirmish—"

"It was more than that."

"But." I chewed on my lip. "I healed Jamie. Assuming it wasn't there until after I enchanted the place into existence—because it wouldn't have worked otherwise—it couldn't have been there by the time they were hurt, either. My powers did flicker a little, but I wouldn't have been able to heal him there if the para-paranormal was present at the time."

"Do we know how that stuff comes into existence exactly?"

I thought over what Ravana had boasted to me. The words came to me almost verbatim, as if bursting up from the recesses in which I'd buried them. "'Dark magic meets dark magic. And produces para-paranormal... as the result of death.'"

"So perhaps it takes at least a few minutes, if not hours, to fully form."

I suppose that would explain why it hadn't been there immediately. "But this just proves what my mom told me. That Eithne could have tampered with the design."

"If the blueprints themselves weren't at fault," Draven added. He really did have a nose for the details.

"Zashil told Roan he'd ask one of Fred's other partners to forward the blueprints. But that would be ridiculous, wouldn't it? Putting a dangerous, real trap in your designs to begin with."

"Still, it's worth examining."

"It wouldn't explain the presence of para-para-normal." I sighed. "What did you do with it?"

"I didn't do anything." Draven cleared his throat. "Faine and I both wanted nothing to do with the stuff. Cable cleaned it for us."

Right. Only humans weren't impacted by it, as far as we knew. "Did he dispose of it?"

"He scraped it into a bucket Faine found for him in the backroom and then scrubbed the rest away."

"But there had to be blood all over the place." I felt numb. Poor Cable.

"He insisted. He didn't want to disturb Roan,

and he didn't want that stuff hanging around where it could do any of us paranormal creatures harm."

The thought of him scrubbing that alone, for our sakes… A flush rose to my cheeks. I'd have to check in on him later. "Where'd he stash the bucket?"

"In the back of the shop, in the empty area they told me Zashil and his partner had had pegged for another room. We didn't know what else to do with it. I didn't want to take it home with me again." He shuddered. He'd done so for me before, and Ravana had stolen it. He'd also witnessed how the gel-like substance had burned permanent scars into her flesh.

"Okay," I said, a yawn escaping me despite the harrowing sense of dread invading me down to my very bones. "We'll ask Roan if he can take it to the woods or something."

"Tomorrow," said Draven firmly.

Mom's cuckoo clock chimed one o'clock down the hall. I reached back and patted Broomie as she slept. "Tomorrow," I agreed. "But be careful—an evil witch is still out there."

"And whatever paranormal creature worked with her to produce the para-paranormal from the man's death." Draven frowned. "So Spindra displayed a slightly troubling interest in the man. Who else might have had a motive to want him dead?"

"You, for one."

Draven scowled. "You dare accuse me, after you suspected me last month?"

I lifted a hand in surrender. "You have to admit I wasn't entirely far off. A vampire *was* the culprit."

His lips pinched tightly together. "I met the man once—for several seconds."

"And he irritated the living daylights out of you." I chuckled blearily at my choice of phrase. "You know what I mean."

"Any man who laid a hand on you would irritate me."

We were getting to *that* again, would we? Though it was true he hardly treated Cable more cordially than he had Fred, and there was a world of difference between the ways both human men had treated me.

"Fine. I apologize. You and Qarinah were asleep when the incident happened anyway." I frowned, thinking it over. "I was with Mayor Abdel—and the mummy wouldn't hurt a fly. So that actually doesn't leave that many suspects." Luna Lane had more paranormal residents than the average town by far. But even just *one* paranormal resident was more than the average town could boast.

"We need to interrogate Spindra," he said plainly.

"*We?*"

He looked irritated. "You, then. While I'm asleep tomorrow and missing everything, as usual." He practically spat the last few words, his Eastern

European accent coming through even thicker than typical.

I jumped as he put both hands on my upper arms, the coldness reaching through my shawl. "But you *need* sleep. You look about to pass out."

"And while I doze, Eithne and her accomplice could be plotting their next murder."

He grunted. "I'll dig up what I can until dawn. Let's confer at sunset again. By then, Roan and Zashil should have more for us."

I nodded, but even that slight movement felt heavy and too much.

"Thank you," I said simply as Draven turned and made his way to the door.

He froze. "You're welcome," he said, his hand on the door handle.

"Be careful," I added.

Flinching, he said softly, "You, too." As he pulled the door open, he popped into his bat form and fled into the night.

I went after him to shut the door, leaning my warm cheek against the solid surface of the wood as I watched his little form flutter away into the darkness, the large, blood-red moon watching down over the town in glee.

Chapter Twelve

*I*n the morning, I enjoyed Faine's company at my little two-seater table beside my kitchen, so often unused that I had to clean away a layer of dust before we began. I was happy to see the enchantment, one of my most go-to ones, caused no trouble at all. A weary day's sleep, a way forward in finding some form of justice for the man, however unpleasant he might have been, had woken me with renewed energy.

"Thank you again," I said, sipping Faine's delicious coffee. "I feel bad taking you away from the café—and the kids! Did the girls get off to school all right?"

Faine chuckled. "It's almost eleven, Dahlia. You slept in. You were sound asleep the first time I swung by, so I made my lunch delivery to Milton and Cable early and came back."

Right. Okay, so I wasn't entirely back to form. "How's he doing?"

"Who? Milton? He doesn't really know what happened. We figure it's best not to tell him. He doesn't remember Fred to begin with."

"Good idea," I said. "But I meant…" I swallowed a large chunk of the cinnamon roll she'd brought me.

"Oh. Cable." Faine's eyes sparkled. "Fine. Worried about you, of course, but I told him you were fast asleep and I'd keep an eye on you today."

"You can't!" I said around mouthfuls of pastry. "Poor Grady, you've stuck him with the café and Falcon now for two days—"

"'Stuck him'?" Faine shook her head. "Dahlia, it's his café and his son, too. He's fine with handling it while I'm there for a friend." She squeezed my elbow. "And after everything you've told me, I've got to know. I won't have another murderer running around Luna Lane. Not after Ravana. Not after what she did to my child." She choked up, and it was my turn to offer her a hug.

"I won't miss signs like that again," I promised. "And nothing will keep me from helping on full moon night."

"Don't be silly." Faine pulled back and wiped away a tear. "That's All Hallows' Eve this month. Don't you have witch rituals to perform?"

Halloween was the big holiday for witches, but

since Mom had died, I'd been a bit lax in the celebrations, simply lighting a candle in a Jack-o-Lantern and saying a prayer to my mother and the witches in our bloodline before her—whoever they might have been.

Now that I knew about what the Poplar family motto translated to, I wasn't sure I regretted not knowing anything about them.

I dry-swallowed. "Faine, Mom told me something else when I summoned her."

"You mean besides the fact that she and Eithne were once friends and that the witch likely had a role in Fred's accident—*murder?*"

That had to be my focus. There was still so much we didn't know about that, and a murderer besides Eithne on the loose was far more pressing.

"She said, 'It's in your blood.' And she was sorry."

"What is? Sorry for what?"

"I… I don't know. But you mentioning All Hallows' Eve just now reminded me how we pray to our witch ancestors."

"And you always got irritated because your mother kept it vague and never mentioned a thing about them."

"Right." I sighed. Mom had been almost perfect in every way—but whatever had driven her here, into the arms of a "friend" who'd wind up stabbing her in the back, had been too harrowing for her to relay. And I'd felt… Like a little bit of me had been missing because of it. "What if something involved in this case went wrong because of some kind of deficiency in my bloodline?" I thought over the dreary Latin Poplar motto. It was used on gravestones. Did my witchy family specialize in putting people beneath the earth? They were proud enough to work the foreboding message into the family crest.

"What do you mean? I thought we decided it was Eithne, not you, whose magic tampered with the blueprints."

"Which I still need to see." I jumped to my feet, stuffing the rest of the cinnamon roll into my mouth and swallowing the last of my coffee. It went down hot, but not hot enough to burn me. "We've got to get going. I've got a busy day, and if you're up for accompanying me…"

"I am, but I'm still confused." She stood and stroked Broomie, who'd stuck her brush in her empty cornhusk bucket and let out a little broomstick sigh.

I needed to feed her—and check in on the Mahajans at the same time.

Once my hat and shawl were on, I kept talking as I slid into my ballet slippers and Faine into her vintage platform heels.

"Whatever Mom was hiding from, whatever could have been worse than Eithne—even if she'd truly trusted her at one time, she was always more of a wicked witch than a benevolent one—perhaps had to do with her family."

Broomhilde slid beside me and nudged her way into my hand.

"Witches who do bad things?" Faine asked as we stepped down my porch and headed across the street to Vogel's. It was closed. It was almost never closed.

"What if I *am* at fault? Unconsciously?" I bit my lip and peered inside Vogel's front window. Broomie moaned forlornly and pointed past the wicked-looking pumpkin that had mocked me the other day to the stack of corn back by the rest of the produce.

"I don't understand," Faine said. "We decided it wasn't a flaw in your construction—that it was a deliberate redesign or an error in the blueprints. A deadly one."

"But Fred irritated *me*!" I admitted, spinning on my heel. When I'd accused Draven of the same thing, I'd nearly forgotten that entirely. There was another paranormal creature in town who hadn't much liked Fred. Who'd had her hands all over the situation. Me!

"And you think you unconsciously built this trap to kill him?" Faine raised an eyebrow.

"I don't know!" I wrung my hands together. "But if I had some ill intent, even just a small one, and Eithne capitalized on that to tweak my enchantment here and there—perhaps that would qualify as dark magic meeting dark magic resulting in death."

Faine studied me as Broomie scraped her bristles against the locked front door. It wasn't opening.

"You wanted Fred dead?"

"Of course not!" I laughed darkly. "He was leaving town anyway. But I was worried about the out-of-towners, and frankly about *him* knowing our secret. So maybe I… Maybe without thinking, I… wished he would just… no longer be a problem."

"But… But, Dahlia. How could you have known he'd even go through that trap? Why put anyone else in danger? Jamie's one of us and he nearly got his leg obliterated." She'd updated me this morning that Jamie was back home, resting. Physically fine, though. County hospital had given him the all-clear. So that was one thing I'd done right at least.

And that was one more person I needed to speak to about what had happened yesterday.

"Maybe… there's more than one death trap in that room," I said, horrified that it hadn't even occurred to me.

Faine took both my hands in hers. "Okay. We'll consider it a possibility. But let's eliminate the other ones first, all right?"

"I should just turn myself in."

"No." Faine shook her head firmly. "Not until we know *exactly* what went wrong."

"Okay," I said quietly. My thundering heart threatened to drown out all energy and sense of purpose I'd woken up with.

"Dahlia, Faine." Arjun shuffled up the sidewalk, likely from his house a block over, his slow pace and empty hands not at all like how he usually started his day. He pulled a set of keys out of his pocket as he approached, his tired eyes indicating he'd gotten far less sleep than I had. "What can I get you?" He smiled just a little as he patted Broomie, who'd floated back slightly to allow him access. "Besides cornhusks?"

"Just the husks today," I said, and Broomhilde was already soaring inside right for the discard bin. It was nearly empty at the beginning of the day, and Broomie swallowed the single husk quickly, popping out from it again with a huff. Arjun shuffled over to her and began peeling the husks off the remaining few ears of corn, though it looked in desperate need of restocking.

"Arjun, should you be working today?" asked Faine. "Is Goldie with Zashil and Javier?"

"Yes," said Arjun. "My son… My son is in a state."

I could imagine. His friend, his business partner, his dream all gone within a single day. If I was the second paranormal creature responsible… I'd never forgive myself.

"Jeremiah has still offered to drive over the produce today," he said. "After he heard what happened, he thought maybe I might want a day off. But no… It must be stocked. The store must be open. People need to shop."

Faine nudged me. "You *have to* do a good deed today." She pointed at the back of my hand. It itched as soon as she reminded me of it, and I tugged on my sleeve to try to cover it.

Bananaberries. She was right. I had no time for this—but Arjun needed me, and I needed to help him anyway.

"Arjun," I said. "You head back to Goldie and Zashil. Let me do the stocking and the running of the shop." I bit my lip and looked to Faine. I needed to talk to people—to Spindra, to Jamie, to Zashil. How could I run the shop all day today?

"No, no, I need to work." Arjun studied me as he handed the husk in his grasp directly to Broomie. She munched it down with relish. "But you can stock, yes. Please help me, Dahlia, with the stocking. Only, please, do not carry too much today?"

"Agreed," I said. Faine and I exchanged a look. We'd continue our task for the day as soon as I finished.

"Here," said Arjun, lifting a pumpkin from the pile beside the door and putting it in my outstretched arms. "A gift. For your help." The smile he offered me didn't reach his eyes.

"Thank you," I said, taking it. I needed a Jack-o-Lantern for Halloween regardless. Only I looked down at it. It was that mocking, pockmarked one. I stuck my tongue out at it, which Arjun might have commented on if he hadn't been so distracted. I hadn't strained myself completing my stocking good deed today, now had I?

"Please consider closing up early today," I told him. Broomie floated near the door, a satisfied little belch escaping between her bristles. "You look like you could use a break."

"You as well, Dahlia." The slight smile on his lips seemed more genuine this time.

I hadn't had the heart to add to his burdens with anything I'd learned so far. But that meant… Well, he had to think my enchantment was at fault, dark magic or not.

And yet he still seemed to forgive me.

I gave him a quick half-hug, the pumpkin jostling between us. "Take care, Arjun."

He seemed about to cry, but he took a deep breath and shuffled back to the counter. "I have my health—and my family. We will get through this. My son has his husband. He will feel better one day."

It seemed like Zashil ought to be the first meeting on my to-do list.

After dropping the pumpkin off at home, I sat on Broomie's shaft and floated across the sidewalk, on my way to the Mahajans'.

"Dahlia!" With an all-too-familiar ragged breathing, Cable popped out from his uncle's front door and headed down the walkway, waving wildly to catch my attention.

"Whoa, girl," I told Broomhilde, sliding down to the sidewalk. She shook her bristles as Cable drew closer, partly out of irritation, but partly to be intimidating, I was sure of it. Sure enough, she let out her little bristly form of laughter as he instinctively drew back a little at her display.

"Thank you," I said before Cable could say anything. "Draven and Faine told me you cleaned up the para-paranormal. At the… the scene."

Cable frowned. "While you were helping Arjun, Faine filled me in. Eithne… and someone else, huh? Murder?"

I wondered if she'd floated my theory that that someone else could have been *me*. From the way he studied me, I'd venture not.

Or he just didn't believe me capable of it, even subconsciously.

"She headed back to the café for a few hours, but she told me to call her when I spotted you about to start your… investigation."

Investigation? That sounded so official, but he wasn't wrong.

I was starting to make a habit of such things.

"I'm headed to speak to Zashil," I said. "See if those blueprints came in."

Cable chewed his lip. "I wonder if you might start with Roan first?"

"Roan?" I asked. "Why?" As far as I knew, he was knee-deep in making up some cover story to explain the dead out-of-towner to any outside authorities.

"Well, Zashil is so upset, and still so close to it.

He promised to get Roan those blueprints, so if that's what you're mostly after, Roan might be in a better frame of mind."

Hmm. He wasn't wrong there. I'd still need to talk to Zashil eventually, but right now, I didn't have any specific questions for him, but I'd want to hear his version of what the game had seemed like behind the scenes. Though he'd already relayed that he hadn't been able to stop the trap door when he should have had control.

"Good idea," I said. "We can call Faine from the sheriff's office."

"*We?*" Cable asked brightly.

"Oh." My face flushed. "You probably have research to do—and your uncle. Sorry. I can call her—"

"No, I'd like to help." He scratched at his stubble-covered chin. "I just didn't think I'd be invited."

"Why not? I could use the help."

Swallowing, he pointed at Broomhilde timidly. "Do I have to ride her?"

She snickered again and bent her handle to pat the bottom of her shaft, as if to invite him along for the ride.

I had a feeling he'd regret it.

But I wasn't about to turn her down for a car ride again. I'd already seen how it had sent her running to Draven, of all people...

I still didn't fully get that.

"I'll meet you there," I said. "Maybe you can swing by the café and get Faine along the way?"

"I'll do that." He pulled a set of keys out of his pocket. "Let me just tell Milton and I'll be on my way."

Milton had been left alone quite a lot before Cable had arrived, though we'd all taken turns checking in on him. He'd be fine. His house was set up to make things easier for him.

Swinging my leg back over Broomie's shaft, I leaned forward and let her zip us down the street.

Chapter Thirteen

*R*oan's computer and monitor were probably about two decades old, but he had the internet and he'd gotten the forwarded emails with the blueprints.

Together, we flipped through them, though neither of us was particularly knowledgeable of what it was we were looking it.

"This is it," said Roan, tapping the screen with a stubby finger. I was sitting in his office chair in front of the computer, and he leaned on the back of the chair, hunched over. In the empty and newly repaired jail cell a few feet over, Broomie was amusing herself with a game she'd made of smacking a crumpled-up piece of paper she'd stolen from the waste bin under the cot and back out again.

I looked at the drawing of the tunnel trap door on the leftmost jail cell. I couldn't exactly tell what material the doors were meant to be made of from this, but I could clearly see there wasn't meant to be anything between one door and the other. No heavy stone-like trap to smush anyone who crawled through.

As we'd thought. Someone had tampered with the design afterward. Whether or not my subconscious's ill intent had been enough to merge with what had to be Eithne's magic and create para-paranormal, I couldn't yet say.

"So all signs point to Eithne," Roan said roughly.

"Yes," I said simply, leaning back. *And me.*

"How are we going to spin this?" Roan let out a huff and sat in a rigid metal chair across from me, where a visitor would usually sit. "There was a mix-up with the material for the door? But why go to the trouble of outfitting the whole tunnel with stone that could drop down and hurt someone?" He sighed, scratching his cheek.

"Then there's the matter of putting the blame on a construction company that has no records of ever doing anything in Luna Lane." I hated to suggest this, but I couldn't let anyone else pay for my mistakes. "What if he got into an accident elsewhere in town?"

Roan frowned but nodded. "That was Mayor Abdel's suggestion, too."

"What would... What would result in those

kinds of injuries?" I wanted to be helpful, but this whole thought exercise made me sick.

"We won't know exactly until I get that coroner's report." Roan shuffled some papers on his desk. "But something that would have to smush the poor man, no doubt."

Yeah, I didn't want to think about it.

I clicked away from the blueprint and leaned back, hugging my shoulders. Faine and Cable were sure taking their time.

Broomie's pit, pit, patter with the little wad of paper echoed out somewhere behind me.

"Roan, I might be—" I started, about to confess my potential guilt, but his voice was louder, his question more pressing.

"How did your mother die, Dahlia?"

My lips snapped shut. "Why would you ask that now?"

"You would never talk about it," said Roan, twiddling his thumbs on his lap. "At least not to me."

"You loved her—"

"She was my *friend*, Dahlia. I knew that we'd never be more. I wanted to know ages ago. I was afraid…" He stared up at the ceiling.

"Afraid of what?"

"That you might have had a role in it—accidentally."

My heart felt as if it had stopped beating. "You… *what?*"

"You said you found her there, in the middle of your rune circle. She either died of a heart attack, as we all thought, or you—or she—cast some enchantment that went wrong. Your mom was relatively young. A heart attack isn't impossible, but…"

"It was an enchantment. But it wasn't her or me. It was Eithne."

"So you seem to have thought all along," Roan said, his voice soft. "I wish you'd told me about the other witch being there. I was afraid… I knew you wouldn't have done anything to your mom on purpose, and I didn't want to bring up that kind of guilt. But it's been eating at me all this time."

"I'm sorry," I said softly. If only he knew about what Mom had hinted, what the Poplar motto portended—the potential for wicked magic in my blood. Maybe he wouldn't have been so wrong to suspect me. "But I wasn't there when it happened."

Roan nodded. "I knew a witch had cursed you before birth, but I never knew about this wicked witch who used to live in town—I moved here shortly before your mother did."

I hadn't known that. I supposed if he'd grown up here, he *would* have known about Eithne and yet it hadn't occurred to me to be angry at him for "keeping" that from me.

"She was there," I said hoarsely. "Standing over my mother's body. I opened the door, and Mom was dead—Eithne just looking down at her, a flask in her hand."

"A flask?"

"Yeah… I screamed at her, and she didn't respond at first. She was frozen, I guess? Almost like she hadn't expected whatever she'd done to work. Then she simply smiled, sat on her broomstick without a word, and flew past me out the door. You know the rest. I didn't keep anything else from you. I promise."

"Why'd you keep that from me?" Roan reached across the desk and put a hand over mine on the computer mouse. "You shouldn't have had to bear such a thing alone."

"I told Faine," I said quietly. "And Draven eventually—I just… I was ashamed, I guess."

"Ashamed?"

I swallowed. "That I hadn't been there. That I hadn't been able to save her. That that wretched witch had taken the last essential part of me away, trying to finish what she'd started before I'd been born."

Roan shifted back into his seat and let my words linger in the air.

"What was in the flask?" he asked.

For a second, it seemed an odd thing to focus on, but with the distance of years behind me… "I asked Mom—her spirit—once. But she'd never tell me. She won't tell me anything important." My chest ached.

"Was it empty or full?" Roan prodded.

"I… Half-full, I guess."

"What color was the potion?"

Why were we focusing on this *now* of all times?

"I… I don't know." I closed my eyes and tried to picture the scene, but my stomach clenched at the sight of the witch with the long, silver hair standing over my mom's body, Broomhannah stiffly still lying across Mom.

"Don't stress yourself," Roan said quickly. "I just thought… Well, if you knew what she'd stolen, why she might have killed your mother, it could help explain what she's still doing in Luna Lane all these years later, visiting you, playing a role in these deaths."

I frowned. He was right, of course. I wished I could look at my mother's murder with an investigative detachment. But it hurt too much.

The door leading to the street opened, and in stepped Faine and Cable. "Sorry we're late. We brought food!"

Of course. I could always count on Faine to keep me fed when my thoughts were scattered elsewhere. As if on cue, my stomach growled.

"Thank you, dear," said Roan, rising to meet them. The smell of turkey and pumpkin pie was impossible to miss. My eyes flit to the computer screen to check the time—it was mid-afternoon, but I'd skipped lunch, so an early dinner would be fine with me—and my gaze caught on the sender of the email with the blueprint attachments.

Karter Wattana.

K.W.

So it had been a business partner who'd texted Fred those things?

What had those texts said?

I didn't know why it mattered, but it was something I felt I needed to know.

"What is it?" asked Cable, the bag in his hand lowering slowly to the desk in front of me.

"Roan, can we call this guy?" I pointed to the screen.

"What guy?" Roan leaned around Cable to inspect the screen, a turkey sandwich already in his hand. "The business partner?"

"Does he know Fred is dead yet?" I asked.

"No," said Roan. "Though I'm sure he knows something isn't quite right. Zashil could barely compose himself when he gave him a call, and there he was, asking for blueprints that Fred should have been able to procure himself."

"It's just…" I worried my bottom lip. I was being silly, right? How were those texts any of my business?

"Spit it out, Lia." Roan tossed his sandwich on a stack of papers on his desk. "No detail is insignificant in an investigation."

So even the town's sole official investigator was making me take point on this.

"I saw something on Fred's phone—I wasn't interested in spying on him or anything, but the first few lines of a couple of text messages popped up when he was trying to show me the blueprints." I pointed to the screen. "They were messages about something being urgent, Fred needing to return the person's calls. And they were from 'K.W.'"

Cable tapped a finger against his chin. "I wouldn't be surprised to find those kinds of messages between business partners. Maybe something came up at one of his other locations."

Faine slipped out of her coat and hung it on the back of the stiff metal chair across the desk. "But what would that have to do with the accident"—she winced—"murder here?"

"Someone else with a dislike for Fred, perhaps?" I suggested. "A motive?"

Roan nodded. "Though the murder would then have to be a hired hit. We'd notice this Karter Wattana here. Strangers never go unnoticed."

A hired hit with a witch and another paranormal creature entirely? Even if he'd known about the witch—which was unlikely, even the likes of Eithne didn't relish paranormal society's existence being widely known—then why drag yet another paranormal person into it? The witch alone should suffice.

Unless… Unless *my* enchantment, my subconscious resentment of Fred, had been enough to act as the second set of dark magic, as I'd worried about since this morning. Then he could have used Eithne alone and the para-paranormal could have simply been the unintended aftereffect of my unwitting involvement in the murder.

"You mentioned reading a message about a problem and K.W. needing to speak with him, nothing about a diatribe of someone who hated Fred enough to kill him," Cable pointed out.

"It's a long shot, but it's worth not ruling out anything early on," said Roan. "Let's at least find out what those messages were about, and what this other franchise partner might be able to reveal about our victim."

I clicked the email and found a telephone number in Karter's signature line. Roan saw what I brought up and picked up his desk phone, dialing. He stood there quite a while and hung up. "His voice mail is full," he said simply. Grabbing his coat off the rack nearby, he stuffed the last few bites of his tossed-aside sandwich into his mouth. "I'll check with Zashil. Find out how he reached him."

"We could reply to the email," said Faine.

Roan nodded. "You do that, sign it with my name so he knows it's official, and meet me at the Mahajans'."

Faine came around the desk and tugged on the back of the office chair I was sitting in. "First Dahlia needs to eat. I'll type it."

I stood to switch spots with her and Cable opened up one of the bags they'd been carrying, handing me a wrapped sandwich.

I uncovered it and took my first bite as Roan headed outside. "*So* good," I said to Faine.

She smiled but didn't look up from the computer screen.

The small sheriff's office went quiet as Broomie kept up her bat, bat, batting of the paper-wad-turned-toy.

"So what do we do next?" Cable sipped from a paper cup likely containing a hot drink.

"You don't want to head to the Mahajans'?" asked Faine.

Cable looked to me, as if it were my call.

I was the one with the most investment in this travesty, but I was still an amateur investigator. I felt like I'd partially *stumbled* on the mystery of what had happened to Leana and the Davises.

"Roan should have that covered," I said, taking another bite of my sandwich. "I wanted to speak with Spindra and Jamie—and I… I should probably see the scene of the crime myself again. Look at it with a set of fresh eyes."

"Well, we'll need Zashil to go look at the escape room," Cable pointed out.

Faine sighed and went back to her typing. "I do so wish the Spooky Games Club had been able to play."

"No, you don't," I said. "Not if there was a trap door that actually resulted in death. Who knows what other deadly disasters are inside? That's one thing I have to investigate. Can you print out those blueprints?" I asked.

"Sure," said Faine. "I just need to click *send* on this email."

Cable and I both enjoyed our sandwiches in relative silence as Roan's rickety old fax-machine-printer combo warmed up and then spit each sheet out, one by one by one.

"So… Are you getting a lot of research done?" I asked, for want of anything else to focus on.

Cable laughed. "Not the past few days, no. But I got enough done over the past few weeks." He sipped from his coffee cup again. "A break's good for the brain, too."

I hoped I could feel calm and content enough to take another one myself someday.

With a little skitter across the linoleum floor, the wad of paper Broomie had been playing with hit the toe of my ballet slipper.

"You hit it pretty far that time, didn't you?" I said, putting the last of my sandwich on the paper bag and bending down to pick up the paper wad for her. She chirruped in response and wagged her handle eagerly, waiting for me to return it.

A word sticking out of the uncovered bit in the middle of the page caught my eye. *Beauchamp*.

"That's how you spell 'Bee-cham,'" said Cable, peering over my shoulder. "It's French, but the British pronounce it differently."

That was Fred's last name. I never would have

guessed that was how he spelled it. I uncrumpled the rest of the paper.

It was official-looking government stationery. The line I'd seen a part of read, "Beauchamp Entertainment Enterprises." It was black and white, like it'd been photocopied—and poorly.

"A fax," I said.

Cable pointed to the pixelated date in the bottom corner. "From two days ago."

"Right when Zashil called his parents with the news that they were coming to town," I added. Had that only been two days ago? It felt like so much longer.

Cable and I scanned the page, his head hovering just above my shoulder, his closeness so tangible, it sent a little shiver down my spine, despite the circumstances.

"Seems standard to me," I said. "Roan must have asked for copies of Zashil and Fred's town hall permits to be sent over."

"Couldn't Abdel send someone over with them?" Faine posited, gathering the blueprints and stacking them.

"It's not from Luna Lane." Cable pointed to the city and county. "It's a construction permit from Creekdale?"

"That's the next town over," said Faine. "Well past the woods, though. Lots of uninhabited space between them and us."

"Ah," said Cable. "I passed through it the other

day. Small town, not so cheery as Luna Lane."

Must have been nice. Going places even as apparently dull as Creekdale.

I folded it up and tucked it into the little pouch at my belt. "Well, so that's another thing to ask Zashil about."

"Were they going to build another escape room in Creekdale?" Faine asked. She frowned as she slipped the stack of papers into her purse. "You'd think they'd have mentioned it. And why so close? Creekdale is close enough that people who live there can come here for any games."

"Maybe they were going to build in Creekdale first?" wondered Cable. "Then switched to Luna Lane? It's not like you have to use a permit once you have it. Franchises might apply in multiple places, see which place responds the fastest."

"Or which place has a witch who can *build* the fastest," I muttered. Broomie nudged at my pouch with a little bristly moan and I realized with a start I'd taken away her new toy. Petting her, I let her know I'd find her a new one—but first, we had places to be, people to interview.

Faine and Cable hustled with cleaning up the packaging from the early dinner they'd brought. I snatched up my sandwich again before they could throw it away, finishing it off in a few bites.

"Tailor's shop or First Taste?" I asked as they met me at the door.

"Jamie's not working," said Faine simply. "He's

fine—physically—but he took a couple of days off to recuperate."

"Then let's swing by the tailor's," I said, our destination decided.

Chapter Fourteen

*S*pindra's Tailor Shop seemed inviting from the outside, a luscious display of ball-gowns and tuxedos in the window, though no one in Luna Lane would likely have need for them very often. The spiderwebs around the headless mannequins could easily be explained away with the black-and-orange décor, the message written in webs like something done by a certain Charlotte reading, "Look Your Best This Halloween."

The rest of the year, the spiderwebs might have seemed out of place. But in the chilly October air, the red and yellow leaves gathering in the gutter at our feet, it seemed a simple harmless marketing campaign.

Spiderwomen were known for seeming harmless when they had a mind to.

The bell rang overhead as Cable opened the door for Faine and me, and I didn't fail to catch the way his Adam's apple bobbed as I passed him by.

"Afraid?" I asked. Broomie snickered in my hand, though I hadn't meant to tease him.

Cable loosened the collar at his neck as the door closed behind him. "She made… Quite an impression when Goldie called her up to sew me some underwear."

"I imagine," I said, remembering how his first night here he'd forgotten to pack his unmentionables.

Oh, Spindra would have had *a time* with that.

"Faine, Dahlia, darlings." Spindra's Slavic accent made her every word more elegant, and the way she sashayed into the shop from behind a black, silky hanging curtain only added to the effect. She usually slept during the day in the back, but she kept her shop open during daytime hours, waking up easily whenever anyone came inside. Her nocturnal instincts were more preference than necessity like the vampires'.

"Cable," she added, slower, as she folded her long fingers together, those black nails like claws she could shred her own skin with.

Cable cleared his throat but took a step back, and Broomie shook again with her little bits of giggling.

"Hello, Spindra," said Faine brightly.

She obviously didn't suspect her of a thing. Or she was better at acting innocent for this investigative stuff than she had any right to be as a chef and Games Club enthusiast.

"Please, come look around. Broomhilde, darling, feel free to search out a piece of yarn or a strip of cloth that might catch your fancy in the back."

Broomie brightened at that, giving me a quick nudge before escaping from between my fingers and flying through the hanging curtain. It had been a while since she and I had been here, but she'd know just where to look.

"Are we looking for something special for All Hallows' Eve?" Spindra was at my side practically before I even realized it, giving a lock of my hair a slight tug as I let out a yelp. "I can see it. Violet. With black stripes. I'd spin it to go perfectly with your hat."

I probably would dress up for Halloween, even if my rituals were done alone, but that was the last thing on my mind right now. "That would be lovely, Spindra, but that's not why we're here."

It wasn't why *I* was here, anyway. Faine was over by the scarves, running her fingers over a long, polka-dotted black-and-white number that would look great with the 1940s-style pin-up girl attire she most often wore.

"Oh?" asked Spindra. She crossed her arms over her chest, cradling one elbow with the other hand, and looked Cable up and down, her gaze settling uncomfortably on his waist area. "Did you lose your underpants again, young man?"

"I never lost them," said Cable gruffly. "Just forgot them." He swallowed under her gaze and quickly turned to look at a display of dress shirts. Any one of them would seem at home in his closet.

"Spindra, we're here to talk about Fred," I said quickly, getting us back on track.

Spindra stiffened. "What of him?" She spoke with such detachment, it was almost forced. Not that she was ever known for any emotion other than "lustful" to begin with.

It was almost enough to send me off-track. I ran my hand over a blouse hanging from a rack beside me. "You and he… seemed close."

She laughed. "I didn't know he existed before two days ago."

"Even so," I said. "He clearly caught your eye."

Spindra glided across the shop, weaving between racks and displays as quiet as a spider to stand behind Cable. He didn't notice her. "*All* handsome men… catch my eye, as you say."

Cable let out a little cry at her nearness and pressed back against the wall, a dress shirt clutched to his chest. His head jostled a suitcoat above his head. It looked familiar.

"That would be a beautiful color on you, darling," said Spindra. She took the shirt from his hands as if she were removing the shirt he actually wore, with slow, careful movements. "But this color is better, yes?" She swapped the shirt for another on the display, holding it out before Cable. Her fingers pressed through the layers of clothing to practically trace the fine lines of the muscles that I figured he had under all those clothes. Though I'd yet to see him working out to justify the way his muscles popped against whatever he wore.

"That suitcoat," I said, my annoyance at how close this gorgeous woman was getting to the merely *visiting* professor who was just *my friend* vanishing as I remembered. "Fred wore it yesterday."

"You have a fine eye, too, I see," said Spindra, reaching up above Cable's head as if he weren't even there.

She brought down the suitcoat. I'd *thought* his coat yesterday had been better made than the one he'd worn the day before. Hand-stitched by our local spiderwoman. I'd overheard them saying as much, but I'd been too busy suppressing my gag reflex to dwell on it.

"That Fred had such fine taste," she said softly, stretching out one of the jacket's arms to look at it. "Only two of these in the world, I told him. This one and the one he…" She stopped, her voice cracking.

Draven was right. She'd definitely been affected by this man's death.

But was it because of guilt?

Faine cleared her throat and readjusted her purse strap over her shoulder. "You didn't find the man… a little forward?" I could tell she'd been trying to phrase it as tastefully as possible.

"Oh, I *love* forward men, darling." Spindra seemed herself again as she curled her hand like a cat's in the air. "They're the most fun to break."

"Break?" Cable's voice came out like a whimper.

"Ha," said Spindra, setting the coat down on a nearby rack. "You break so easily, darling, you may as well be made of glass. That's hardly as much fun." She winked at him. "You're safe."

Safe? Poor choice of words, considering.

"Spindra, were you making out with Fred behind the shoe rental counter?" I asked. "In the old bowling alley before I converted it?"

"Yes." She threaded her hands together, her straight, black hair falling jaggedly over one silver eye. "Is that a crime?" She looked from me to Faine to Cable and back. "Are you asking if I played a role in his accident?"

"It wasn't an accident," I said quickly.

Spindra's visible eye widened, but she didn't otherwise even flinch.

I continued. "Dark magic was at play—and the presence of a second paranormal."

"Dark magic? You mean Eithne?" Spindra lifted an eyebrow. "I've heard of her, but she left before I moved in." That was true. Spindra had arrived in Luna Lane when I'd been a child. That didn't mean Eithne couldn't have introduced herself after she'd left town. She'd appeared at my house just last month. "Or could it have been *you*?" Spindra ventured. "Seems to me, darling, you had the most opportunity to tamper with any of the construction. I didn't see Eithne there."

"Dahlia isn't a murderer!" said Faine fiercely, stepping closer to my side.

"And neither am I, darling. Not anymore," she added quietly. "I would never have moved here if I'd thought I could devour a man again." She bristled, jutting her chin up. "I am quite capable of enjoying the art of seduction without eating my prey these days, thank you very much. Mayor Abdel can attest to his faith in me."

"Seems like he had faith in that Ravana, too, and we know what she was up to." Cable didn't seem to expect the attention his comment brought, with all three of our heads turning to focus on him. He scratched his temple and shifted his eyes downward.

"He has a point," I said, but before Spindra could say more, I cut her off. "I'm not saying you had anything to do with his death. I just want to know everything you know about him, hear what you were doing when he died—about ten minutes after the crowd dispersed after the construction was complete."

"I didn't realize Sherriff Roan had hired three deputies, but fine, I will play your little game. I have nothing to hide." Spindra pouted her lips but sashayed back to the counter. "I walked here to my shop, about to turn in for the rest of the day. I couldn't have been here more than a minute or two before I heard the commotion, the crowd returning and dashing down the street."

"Can anyone verify your whereabouts?" Cable asked.

She lifted a brow. "I walked with Jeremiah and Erik as far as my shop," she said simply. "After that… Well, Virginia was here in the shop."

"Virginia?" That was the last name I'd expected to come up.

"Oh, and Broomhilde!" she cried. "Darling Broomhilde, come out, will you?"

Virginia and… *Broomie*?

My mind raced over the details. Virginia had been in a huff before the construction had begun because I'd almost forgotten about her being inside. And Broomie had flown off a while later just before I'd gotten in Mayor Abdel's car.

But Broomie had been in Draven's basement not too long after that, likely having flown in through his bat door.

The hanging curtain jostled and Broomie came out, a long cord of white fabric wrapped around her brush.

"Broomhilde," said Spindra simply, "confirm to your nosy witch that you saw me here, shortly before the ruckus outside and everyone started whispering about Fred's accident?"

Broomie shook her brush up and down as if to say *yes*.

I cocked my head. "And Virginia was here as well?"

Broomie nodded again, her strip of fabric fluttering to the side of her head.

Spindra beamed and walked over to her, tying the fabric strip into an even white bow where Broomie's brush met her shaft. "There," she said. "Lovely."

Broomie perked up, then bent her brush inward slightly, as if shy.

"Broomie, why did you come here?" I asked. Stupid question. Of course she couldn't answer. "Did you come here to find Spindra?"

Broomie shook her head *no*.

"Virginia, then?" Faine asked.

She shook her head *yes*.

"Did you know she'd come here?" I asked.

Broomie replied *no* in her own way once again. The tip of her handle stroked the bow, as if she were in awe of it.

"She likely flew past here on her way to your home," said Cable.

Broomie froze and looked at him, probably deciding whether or not to tease him. But she nodded.

"There you have it," said Spindra. "Your own pretty little pet can vouch for me."

I'd never completely pegged Spindra for the second paranormal creature responsible, but she *had* killed before she'd come here—she'd justify it as the natural way of her kind, but murder was murder—and there had been her intense interest in Fred. She wouldn't even need a personal motive other than to devour him.

But… Squishing the man flat and letting the authorities cart his body away wouldn't have let her eat him.

I sighed. The death hadn't been a spider-woman's m.o. at all.

"Why were you looking for Virginia, Broomie?" Cable asked.

She floated over to me, settling in my hand, but she probably wasn't ignoring him. She just wouldn't know how to answer him.

"Because I offended you both?" I asked. "Misery loves company?"

Broomie nodded. It had been as simple as that.

"Broomie, why did you go to Draven afterward?" I asked. I tried to think of how to word it.

Spindra was able to shed some clues on that. "We three went outside during the commotion, and Erik was the one who told us there'd been an accident at the escape room. Virginia was upset… Perhaps my English isn't so perfect," she said, though I hardly found that to be the case at all. "But she kept on babbling. She said something… 'Cheating'… 'Cutters'?"

"Cheaters?" Faine offered.

We in the Games Club knew how Virginia felt about cheaters. She carried on about even the slightest indication that someone wasn't playing precisely by the rules, whether they'd meant to cheat or not.

"No, not cheating, no…" Spindra snapped her fingers. "Cutting corners. Yes. Whatever that means."

"It means taking shortcuts," Cable explained. "And usually to disastrous results."

"So Virginia probably thought my enchantment was cutting corners—and had led to disaster," I said solemnly. She wasn't wrong.

"She seemed so excited about the escape room, though," Faine pointed out. "She knew you were using magic to construct it."

"Perhaps she didn't view it as cutting corners until disaster happened," said Cable.

Right. Back to the truth of the matter—that it was at least partially my fault. Though Virginia herself had tried to soothe me afterward.

"And Broomie?" I asked.

Spindra shrugged. "She flew off, yes, toward the vampires' manor. But I would not have guessed that was where she was headed. I assumed she was off to find you."

Broomie cooed in my hand, shuddering a little.

"Where's Virginia?" Cable asked. "I haven't seen her since before the construction."

"I saw her last night. She found me in the woods and tried to cheer me up." I grimaced. "I guess even if she viewed it as cutting corners, she didn't think as negatively of it as she does cheating."

"I left her on the street," Spindra said simply. "And went off with Erik to see what had happened. Do I need to tell you all about Erik, too?"

"No," I said quickly. "We've taken up enough of your time." I gestured at Cable, nearest the door, to head out that way.

"Oh, but you did not ask," said Spindra as Faine and I lined up behind Cable, whose hand rested on the door. "About when I met Fred," she said.

She was off my list of suspects, more or less, but anything she had to add could only help. "Yes, of course. He came in to buy the other coat?" I pointed to the burgundy suitcoat she'd left on the rack.

"Yes. He was so *charming*, so not at all intimidated by me." Her succulent lips curled up in a grin. "I am used to being intimidating."

"Charming?" Faine muttered under her breath.

It took all kinds.

"What did you talk about?" I asked, clearing my throat. "When you weren't flirting, of course."

"Oh, there was much flirting," said Spindra, her eyes sparkling wickedly. "And much kissing."

Already? Wow, she'd worked fast.

"I didn't hear the bell over the door," she said. "Because there would have been no need for her to open it. But there she was, gasping and looking away like a little schoolgirl."

"She?" Faine asked.

"Virginia?" I ventured. Who else would gasp at the sight of two adults making out in a relatively public place?

"Yes, Virginia," said Spindra simply. "That was why she returned the next day. She'd wanted to request my services the day before but could not stand to *intrude*, as she so called it."

"Ginny wanted *your* services?" Faine asked. Smart question. What use did a ghost have for new clothes? Besides, she was able to summon accessories at will. Surely, if she'd had intentions of updating her wardrobe at last, she could just *imagine* it into spectral being?

"We talked very little of her request," Spindra said. "I was only here a minute or two before the commotion drew us all outside. But she was still very… *cross*, you might say?"

"Angry?" I supplied for her.

"Yes."

"Well, she left the escape room in a tizzy," said Faine. "That's not too new for her, is it?"

"No," agreed Spindra. I knew I was far from the only Luna Lane resident Virginia "haunted." She loved to gossip and chat with just about anyone. You didn't have to be close to her to be familiar with her moods.

"Thank you for your help," I said. "Anything else you think we should know?"

"No," said Spindra, yawning. "You will tell

Roan everything? I am far too tired to be bothered to repeat myself again."

"Sure," I said.

She spun on her heel and glided through the hanging curtain.

Chapter Fifteen

*W*e stood in front of Spindra's shop, conferring.

"What do you think?" Cable asked. Both he and Faine looked to me—as if I actually were Roan's deputy.

"I think she actually... liked him," I said, as strange as it seemed. It would explain her small cracks of emotion just as much as guiltiness would. "And her alibi seems solid."

"Should we confirm with Erik and Jeremiah?" Faine asked.

I shook my head. "Only if we need to."

"So Jamie's next?" she asked.

"Yeah..." I chewed on the inside of my cheek. "I wonder what Virginia wanted at Spindra's."

Faine stared at the Halloween fancy dress display. "We'll have to ask her. But is that relevant, do you think?"

"I doubt it," I admitted. Broomie shook in my hand. "But it just seems… strange."

Virginia hadn't shown her face around any of us all day. I supposed that meant she hadn't found anything in the remains of Eithne's cabin—or she hadn't bothered looking. She *had* seemed annoyed by the fact that I'd even ask. I'd have to look myself.

But one issue at a time.

"Where does Jamie live?" I asked Faine. In a small town, we all knew the basics about each other, but I wasn't at all close to Jamie. I knew he worked at First Taste, that he was a normie… That was about it. I wasn't a pub person generally. And it had reminded me of Draven for too long.

"I'll lead the way," said Faine, heading down the block. "Qarinah asked me to drop off his check once when he was ill," she explained. "She didn't want to wait until after sunset, in case he needed his rest."

And Faine had no doubt jumped on the chance to bring him some chicken noodle soup.

We followed Faine away from the downtown area, past a collection of quaint houses, and to a large, colonial-style house I knew to be divided into four rooms for rent, with shared common spaces inside.

"Oh, he's one of Doc Day's tenants?" I asked. How could I not have known this?

Doc Day's husband had passed some years back, her kids having long ago moved out. I knew she'd taken on tenants—boarders, she sometimes called them—more to fill up an empty house than to earn extra cash since she didn't charge much.

"Convenient. We can get her take on his state of mind," said Faine. She knocked.

It wasn't long before Doc Day herself answered the door. She smiled through the glass panes decorating the door.

"Hello," she said. "Here to check on the patient?"

"Yes," I said quickly. It sounded better than we were here to unofficially interrogate him. "How's he doing?"

"Much better than expected, considering." The doctor offered to take our coats and shawl as we stepped inside. She lingered to squeeze my hand, the collection of garments over her other arm. "You did amazing work, kiddo."

If only.

"Have a seat." She pointed to her living room, complete with three-quarter sectional and giant TV. "Let me call him down," she said, heading up the stairs.

I set Broomie on the corner of the sectional, and she chirruped as she curled up like a cat, taking special care to put her big bow on prominent display. It kept sticking in her bristles and she'd have to shake her brush to work it free, but eventually, it hung perfectly, and she seemed satisfied.

The three of us sat down, the couch making little rude noises as we settled onto the leather.

"Hey." Jamie shuffled into the room, his hands tucked into his pockets. He was wearing sweats and a long-sleeved T-shirt, his hair a mess, his face long.

"Hello, Jamie," said Faine cheerily. Cable and I said *hi* as well, and Jamie shuffled into the room, sitting down on a recliner across from us.

"Tea, anyone?" Doc Day offered, taking her glasses off and letting them rest against her chest on their chain.

Cable perked up. "Yes, please." He stood and his gaze fell over the room, landing pointedly on me before turning back to Doc Day. "Let me help you with that."

Despite her protests, Cable insisted. "It's the least I can do after all your help with Milton." Soon, it was just Faine, Broomie, Jamie, and I sitting before a giant turned-off TV in a large living room. I had a feeling perhaps Cable thought the young man would be more eager to talk around us, since we at least knew him better.

But no one was talking at all. I looked around. When it was sunnier, I imagined the light would hit this room quite strongly, but it was closer to evening at this point. Perhaps no one watched TV during the day.

"Thank you," said Jamie. He rubbed his nose and sniffled, tapping his knee. "For saving my leg."

"You're welcome." I swallowed. I felt ashamed to be thanked for doing so little to fix a mess I'd had a part in creating.

"How are you feeling?" Faine ventured softly.

A sigh escaped Jamie's lips. "I should say 'fine'— and I am. But every time I close my eyes…" He did just that then and shuddered, opening his eyes and fixing his gaze on his socked feet.

"Jamie, I hate to ask you this, but we need to know what happened." I shirked under Jamie's stare. I could tell what he *thought* had happened. I'd made a mistake somewhere in casting the enchantment.

"It wasn't Dahlia's fault," said Faine simply. "And it was no accident."

Jamie did a double take at that. "What do you mean?"

My mouth felt dry. But it wasn't like we'd taken pains to conceal our theories from the rest of the town. Word would spread like wildfire soon enough. "Do you know about Eithne?" I asked.

"The bad witch," said Jamie. He rubbed one of his upper arms. "I've heard about her, yeah. Almost like a legend around here."

Even in a town with paranormal residents, we still had spooky legends.

"I think—no, I *know* she was involved," I said quickly. "But so was someone else. Someone else who was paranormal."

A twitch in his jaw seemed at odds with the surprise in his eyes. "I see…" was all he said.

"You see?" Faine asked.

"Was I the target?" Jamie asked. "Or Fred? Or both…? Though I wouldn't know who'd want us both dead."

I hadn't even thought to wonder if Jamie had been the intended target, if the murder had gone off a bit. "Is someone after you?" I asked.

"No. I mean…" Jamie fidgeted in his chair. "I feel… Sometimes I feel like something is *watching* me, you know? That feeling was especially strong during the game at one point, but I brushed it off. I'm probably wrong. I don't think anyone has any beef with me."

"Any paranormal person in particular give you an 'off' feeling?" I asked.

Jamie rubbed his nose, sniffing. "Besides Draven?" He laughed, but it was forced.

"Tough boss?" Faine asked.

He shrugged. "I don't know. He can be all right. I just don't particularly like the bloodbag donation policy." He pointed to two faded circular scars on his neck. "I didn't mind giving to Ravana—she was why I wanted to work there to begin with—and Qarinah's pretty fine, too. It's just… awkward with a guy is all." He cleared his throat.

"Don't let him force you," I said quickly. "Boss or not."

"No, he doesn't." Jamie's gaze shot up quickly to meet me in the eye. "It's just… I feel bad giving to the ladies and not him when he won't drink from women, so he has fewer volunteers. So maybe, sometimes, when I turn a corner, I think I catch him looking at me. Like a snack he can't have." He trembled. "But he never says anything, not since I told him *no* the first time he asked."

Faine and I exchanged a look. Apparently, Draven didn't like to drink from women because… because he still thought of it like some kind of betrayal of me. So maybe he went around a little extra thirsty. But I didn't want to get into it here. It seemed irrelevant.

"Draven and Qarinah have an alibi. The… *incident* happened during daylight," I said, redirecting the conversation. "But we're pretty sure Fred was the target. I don't see why the trap door would wait for you to crawl out before it struck down if you were the one someone wanted dead."

"Well, they waited until I was *almost* out." He pointed to his knee.

I winced. True. But as to whether or not that had been an accident or an acceptable casualty to whoever had wanted Fred dead, we'd have to see.

Doc Day and Cable returned then, the latter holding a tray with delicate white porcelain teacups.

"I hope everyone likes chamomile," Doc Day said once Cable had put the tray down. "Good for the nerves," she added, pouring the first cup and handing it to Jamie.

Once everyone was settled—the doctor choosing to stand back in the threshold—and cradling a cup, I decided it was best to see if we could hear his full account of that day.

"I'm sorry to have to ask you this, but can you tell us what happened? No detail is too small."

Jamie's cup rattled in his hand against the saucer.

"Everything seemed normal for the first fifteen minutes or so," said Jamie. "I've done escape rooms before—not this one, but a couple of similar ones, down to crawling through a trap door." I wondered if that was common in the escape room business, similar designs. Did they design their own or hire some experts who contracted out to different franchises? "Fred and I…" Jamie licked his lips. "Well, he was mostly just observing, since as he kept saying, he'd done this room at his other locations before." Jamie stopped to take a sip of tea.

"Were you able to solve a lot of puzzles without any help?" I asked.

"Most escape rooms do offer a hint system," said Jamie. "This one was supposed to offer three hints per game, though we didn't get far enough to ask for even one of them."

"How do you ask for hints?" Faine asked. She leaned forward, the Games Club devotee in her clearly at the forefront.

"For this game, all the members of your team have to agree and you all have to raise a hand. There actually was a point at which Arjun and Goldie were shouting that they wanted a hint, but Fred encouraged me to let them think it through longer, so neither of us raised our hands from inside our cell."

"What puzzle was that for?" I asked.

Jamie shook his head. "I don't know. Ours was the last cell to open, and we only had access to half of a puzzle in our room. I had to shout across the little window with bars on the door to Arjun, who had the other half. Hmm."

"*Hmm?*" I parroted.

"Well, Fred was talking non-stop, but he did pause when I read out the puzzle and my half of the solution."

"Why would he do that?" Faine asked.

Jamie slouched. "He cackled and told me, 'You got it wrong, son,' and I thought I'd blown the interview for sure, even if I know that's silly now, that it wouldn't have all rested on me getting the puzzle right on my first try, but Arjun shouted out his own half of the solution and it worked. The door unlocked with Goldie and Javier's help. They were out of their own cell by then."

I'd bet Fred hadn't been apologetic for getting the puzzle wrong.

"Is that normal for these things? Separating the

players?" asked Cable. He put his teacup down on the end table in front of us. "They're popular enough back home, but I haven't been to one."

Anytime Cable reminded me that his home was elsewhere—so far, far away—something squeezed at my chest.

"Not usually," said Jamie. "But it's definitely not unheard of. There are all kinds of gimmicks you see repeated in escape rooms once you've done enough of them. Sometimes there are things to focus on that a gamemaster will reset for each group, like a pile of kitty litter, sand, or fake dust covering up a clue. You can usually spot those because there's a trail where the mess was shifted in previous games. As far as separating a group, well, I've done prisons and dungeons and the like before—like I said, several rooms with trap doors, including a medieval dungeon that, other than the décor, was kind of like this 'secret prison' one. That was just outside of Creekdale." Jamie scratched his chin in thought.

Creekdale? Like where Zashil and Fred had planned to maybe open a different location? Another escape room nearby—especially a similar one—didn't seem like the smartest business decision. Perhaps that was part of why they'd shifted to Luna Lane.

"Anyway, Arjun and Goldie seemed to be having a time of it out there. Having fun but not knowing what to do. Javier had a better eye for puzzles."

Jamie's knee bounced. "Fred apologized that I didn't have much to do in this cell, but he promised once we were all free, we'd be out there in the main 'guards' area' determining how to escape the prison entirely together."

I hadn't touched my tea yet, so I took a careful sip now. The liquid was lukewarm. "And Arjun sprang the trap door?" I asked, setting my cup down on the table.

"Supposedly," said Jamie. "Though Fred was explaining—he was still treating it like a job inter-view of sorts—that it was actually Zashil in the back hitting the command to pull up the two doors as soon as Arjun had the right solution and hit the button."

"Did anything seem off about the trap door?" Faine asked.

"Well…" Jamie set his own cup down. "As soon as I got in the room, I noticed the panel for the door looked different from the rest of the wall, so I knew whatever it was, it would come into play. I knocked on it, though, and it seemed pretty solid—as solid as the rest of the cell. But Fred didn't notice that, I don't think. He was amused I'd found the trap door right away. So I brushed off the difference in sound, figuring he knew better than I did."

"What do you mean, a difference in sound?" Doc Day asked. I'd almost forgotten she was there.

"The plywood," I answered for him. "If the trap

doors were the relatively harmless material they were supposed to be—"

"When I knocked, there should have been a hollow echo," Jamie confirmed.

"So the room was already deadly before the game began?" Faine asked quietly. "It wasn't changed the moment they crawled through there."

"I suppose not," I said softly. But that didn't mean too much. Only that Eithne and her co-conspirator weren't necessarily present at the time of murder. I'd held on to some hope that my work had been tampered with after I'd left, but this just confirmed I could have been the unwitting second conspirator.

"The trap door opened, and it grinded, as if something heavy were being lifted." Jamie sighed. "I thought it was just sound effects."

"You went in first," Cable said.

Jamie nodded. "Fred insisted. He was taking a very hands-off, observational approach to the whole thing. Made sense."

"Did you notice anything while crawling through the tunnel?" I asked.

Jamie thought for a moment. "I don't think so. But it was just a matter of ten seconds or so to crawl from one end to the other."

"Not wide enough of a tunnel for more than one person to crawl through at once," said Cable.

"No," Jamie confirmed. "But I think Fred started before I was fully out—well, I know he did now." He grimaced. "I couldn't see behind me when crawling through, but Fred's voice got louder, kind of echoing, as I neared the end."

Hmm. "I wonder if the trap activated automatically as soon as Fred was inside?" I asked.

"Automatically?" asked Faine.

"It would explain why Jamie got caught up in it instead of the perpetrator waiting for him to clear the scene. And why there was no one unexpected fleeing the scene right afterward."

"So an alibi for when the incident took place wouldn't really matter that much," said Cable.

Were we back to square one?

"Can they do that?" asked Jamie. "Tailor the trap to a specific person?"

"I think so," I said. "Witches more skilled than I can do a lot with their enchantments."

"Why bother, though?" asked Faine. "Surely, Eithne could just zap someone dead if she so wished —or was commissioned to."

I flexed my left hand, the skin crackling at the edges of the giant stone scale. "Because Eithne likes to be amused." And somehow her desire for entertainment had made it so she'd fooled my mother into being her friend, getting her right where she'd needed to be to curse me.

"You're *sure* Fred was the target?" Jamie swallowed visibly.

Was this kid doing something illegal on the down-low or just paranoid?

"If you were the target, it would have gotten you when you'd still been in the tunnel," I said. "Not wait until Fred was inside and only your leg was still in there."

And judging by the way Jamie had described things to me, I didn't think there could be any mistake. Fred was the target. Jamie was collateral damage.

"What was Fred talking about?" Cable asked Jamie. "Up until he…"

"Died?" Jamie choked on a little sob but tried to play it off. "To be honest, I found myself kind of tuning him out half the time. He'd start talking about something interesting and then…"

"Go on and on about how great he and his ideas were?" I ventured.

"Yeah," Jamie said softly. "But I was *trying* to pay attention in case anything came up again as part of the interview. It's just that… Once I was in the tunnel, it got hard to hear him. He was talking and then there was this loud sound, like one of those chain-held drawbridges in medieval movies getting let loose. It drowned out everything he was saying. Neither of us had time to scream and then— boom." He slapped his hands together.

"Can you remember anything he was talking about at all?" I asked. I wasn't sure how it might be relevant, but if he was so keen to explain the mechanics of the place, it was odd he hadn't noticed the tunnel was off to begin with.

Jamie stared down at his teacup for a while. "A lot about how he's expanding Spooky Escape Rooms, how he has to get going while the going's hot—he outright said he doesn't think they'll be as popular in a decade and by then, he'll be on to the next thing."

"Sounds like a real escape room enthusiast," Doc Day said sarcastically.

I frowned. Zashil had seemed to hope this would be a career for him. Maybe he was simply more optimistic or he only meant for the next few years.

"By the time I was crawling through the tunnels, he was talking a lot about how he doesn't come up with puzzles himself. He contracts out for it with… I want to say, Cameron? Kevin?"

"Karter?" I ventured.

"Yeah." Jamie pointed at me. "That was it."

So that was why this Karter had had the blueprints. He wasn't another franchise manager or owner at all.

"This Karter has designed for a bunch of escape rooms," Jamie said. "But he and Fred went way back, apparently. He used to help him design in college."

"Design what?" I asked. When Fred had been in college, I was pretty sure escape rooms hadn't been a thing anywhere.

"I don't remember." Jamie chewed his lip. "He was talking so fast. Well, but then he kind of choked on his words at one point." Jamie went quiet, thinking for a moment. "Yes. Yes, I remember thinking he talked so much, he'd need a glass of water and then—chains grinding and boom. But he was still talking about him and Karter in the old days when he went through the tunnel, I'm sure. Something... Something about a shed?"

"A... shed?" I asked.

Jamie shrugged. "*Prefab*, I remember him saying that. But I don't know exactly."

Well, prefab sheds had nothing to do with escape rooms, so maybe the man had just been blathering. I stood quickly. We still had to meet up with Roan and touch base with Zashil. "If there's anything else you can remember, let Roan know."

A deep exhale escaped past Jamie's lips. "I don't know if I can ever do an escape room again."

Faine offered him a pat on the shoulder as we all stood and made our way to exit. I whistled to wake Broomie, and her brush lifted before she scurried up into my outstretched hand.

"I'm sorry," I said. "I wish I could enchant the awful memory away."

"Can you?" Jamie looked hopeful.

It was my turn to sigh. "No. I'm sorry. I'm not skilled enough."

He sunk back into his chair. "I understand."

But as he stared off at the blank TV in front of him, his face forlorn, I couldn't help but wish that I could focus on helping people with enchantments—

and that I actually had time to become more skilled at them.

I flexed my left hand, adjusting to the feel of the cool stone on my skin. Until I was sure I wouldn't harm someone again, though, it wasn't going to happen.

Chapter Sixteen

*T*he Mahajans lived at least a fifteen-minute walk from Doc Day and her boarders. Broomie sidled underneath me, and I slipped onto her shaft. "Do you mind if I go ahead?" I asked Cable and Faine.

They exchanged a look and Cable shrugged. "You two can ride Broomhilde if you want."

Faine flushed. "Oh, no." She scratched her ear with her nails in a rather animal-like gesture. "Canines don't do well in high places."

She'd only ever once ridden on Broomie and that had been when we'd been kids. She'd sworn never to again.

And we all knew how Broomie and Cable got along.

"We'll catch up," said Cable, stuffing his hands in his coat pockets.

I offered them both a smile and my thanks for

their help so far, then mounted my broom and took off to the skies above Luna Lane.

The sun was descending on the horizon. I'd be checking in with Draven soon, but I just needed to talk to Zashil first, find out if Roan had gotten a hold of Karter Wattana.

After just a couple of minutes, Broomie descended in front of the Mahajans' house, a cozy, split-level brick ranch with a vegetable garden in the front that mostly just provided Goldie food with which to do her cooking. In the driveway, there were two extra cars in addition to the blue sedan I knew to belong to Goldie and Arjun. Would Javier and Zashil each need their own cars in a town as small as Luna Lane? Then again, it seemed unlikely they'd stick around after all that had gone wrong. Perhaps one of the cars had belonged to Fred. Neither seemed showy enough, though.

Goldie or Arjun had started putting up the Halloween decorations, a Jack-o-Lantern much friendlier than the one I'd likely be carving from my pumpkin beside the front door.

Broomie in one hand, I knocked with the other.

Goldie answered the door, her fingers clutching a white wrap with numerous tassels that ran over her shoulders. "Dahlia, dear." She stepped back, her footsteps heavy-footed, her face drawn. "Come inside."

"How are you all doing?" I asked. Broomie

shook in my hand and Goldie pet her softly, almost absentmindedly, as she shut the door behind me.

"We will get through this," she said. "I feel sorriest for Fred's loved ones—though Zashil and Karter both insist he had so few."

"Karter?" I asked.

"Yes, he's here. The sheriff is speaking to him."

Karter Wattana? Was here in Luna Lane?

My grip tensed around Broomie. "We have to be quiet now," I told her in a whisper.

Grumbling, she settled against the wall near the umbrella stand. For good measure, I removed my witch hat and hung it on the hook behind the door.

"A Halloween decoration if he asks," suggested Goldie simply.

I nodded, smoothing down my wavy hair.

Though I'd been here plenty of times before, Goldie, the ever-gracious hostess, led me down the hallway, through the beaded curtain, and into the family room, which sunk into the ground, accessible by a few carpeted steps downward.

Javier and Zashil were in the nearby kitchen, Zashil sitting at the counter, his back to his husband, who was making something that smelled awfully good. Roan and Arjun sat in a couple of plush chairs in the middle of the family room across from an Asian man who had to have been Karter Wattana. He was dressed in a simple gray suit, but it was rumpled, like he'd been sleeping in it, his tie loose at the collar. His short, black-and-silver hair stuck up in several places in the back, like he hadn't bothered to comb it.

"Friends since college?" Roan asked him, tapping a pen to a pad of paper.

"Yes," said Karter curtly. He turned as I entered and took me in, though his gaze didn't linger uncomfortably long like the gaze of his partner—client? Friend?

"Dahlia," said Roan, gesturing for me to sit beside him. I did, crossing my legs at the ankle nervously, which reminded me suddenly of Virginia, whom I still needed to check in with.

Karter looked to Arjun and Roan, as if waiting for one to provide an explanation.

"Oh, this here is Dahlia Poplar," said Roan, patting my shoulder. Karter's eyes seized on the silver mark on the back of my hand and I moved to cover it with my right hand awkwardly. "She, uh, worked with Fred and Zashil a bit on the escape room setup before Fred's tragic piano moving accident."

Despite myself, I raised a slight brow at Roan. That was what we were going with? Really?

"He was walking by on the sidewalk while someone else was having a piano moved to a second-floor apartment, of course," said Roan, clearing his throat.

Okay, then.

Karter's lips thinned, but he nodded at me curtly. I wondered if he'd already questioned the cause of Fred's death or he was biding his time. "Are you the 'source' Fred kept mentioning?"

"The source?" I parroted back.

Karter let out a sigh and wrung his hands. "To be frank… Fred and I, we're in—I'm in now, I suppose—a bit of trouble."

The text messages about calling him urgently. Karter's own full voice mail.

"I didn't know," said Zashil so quietly from behind Karter, it was almost like he hadn't spoken at all.

"He didn't seem worried to me," added Roan.

Karter looked nauseous. "That's not surprising. Fred's way of dealing with problems is—*was* to ignore them and move on to the next big thing. Always chasing the next big payday that'll fix all of his problems. Then when he catches a break, he sees it as an opportunity to invest in the next, bigger payout instead of making amends. It just never ends." He was turning his hands white now from all the wringing. He let out a dark chuckle. "I guess it ends now. I don't… I don't have the drive he does. I can't keep moving forward."

"What kind of trouble, if I may ask?" Roan's pen tapped, tapped, tapped against his notepad, the kitchen fan whirring as a constant background noise.

Karter blinked rapidly, his dark eyes growing tight. "I suppose it'll all come out soon enough. We were in some… copyright trouble."

"Copyright trouble?" Arjun asked. He gazed over Karter's head to his son, who looked as surprised as his father.

"And what does that mean?" Roan asked, unflustered.

"I design for multiple escape room franchises," said Karter. "I was in the business at the fringes, so to speak, before Fred decided it was the next big thing to get into."

We waited for him to continue, and Javier turned off the fan, perhaps so we could all hear better or maybe because he was about finished. He didn't call anyone over to dinner, though.

"That's why when Zashil told me a sheriff's department needed to look at our blueprints for the Creekdale design, I panicked. I assumed it had to do with the pending case. Fred wasn't answering my calls, so I decided to make my way here and talk to him in person." He choked up. "I never imagined…"

That his foolish friend was as flat as a pancake?

"Wait a minute," I pointed out, reaching into my pouch to pull out the faxed permit from Creekdale. "You said 'Creekdale designs,' not Luna Lane?"

Karter dry-coughed. "They're the same designs. For the most part. Just some… minor adjustments."

Zashil walked closer to take a look at what I had in my hand. Roan didn't seem surprised to see it at all, but it had been in his waste bin, presumably.

"We were originally going to open in Creek-dale," Zashil said. "Leased a location and everything. But just last week, Fred got… strange."

"Strange?" Roan prodded.

Goldie spoke up. "You were going to move to Creekdale? You didn't tell us that!"

Zashil and Javier exchanged a look. Javier stood over a large glass pan containing a steaming casserole. "It would have been a surprise," said Javier. "Once we'd found a place, we would have invited you over."

"Fred and I were both originally from Creek-dale," said Karter. "It made sense he'd want to open there."

From Creekdale? Hadn't Fred just said he'd "spent some time" there in his youth? Odd.

I looked at the permit in my hand. "So what changed?"

Karter cleared his throat but didn't offer anything.

"Fred said we were moving too slow. He didn't blame me, of course, but he just needed his next location up and running. He got especially frazzled when some guy showed up one day. He didn't tell me what they discussed, but he came back and told me, dead serious, we needed to pick a new location and open fast or he couldn't make it happen." Zashil frowned. "That was when I had the idea of asking Dahlia—"

"To offer her construction consulting services,"

Roan said quickly.

Zashil coughed. "Yes, right. And opening in Luna Lane. Fred got excited about the place, how we could buy a location instead of leasing, own it outright—"

"Where did he get the money for all of this?" Arjun asked. "If he was, as you say, in debt, Karter."

Karter shifted uncomfortably, sitting on the edge of his chair. "The money didn't exist, really. It was all new loans to pay the last ones off, promised revenue shares, a third mortgage on his house and his few other properties…"

"So Zashil might not have gotten paid?" Goldie asked, clutching her husband by the shoulder.

"Well, probably he would have." Karter scratched a cheek. "A salary anyway, but any revenue share he promised—Fred would probably think he could talk Zashil out of collecting, promise better returns if he allowed the funds to invest in his next venture."

"Sounds like a lot to keep track of," I said, my mind spinning.

"It was, and that was where we slipped up… Where he—I—slipped up," said Karter. No one said anything in response, so he sighed and continued, turning to face Zashil. "The man who visited him in Creekdale, that was probably the owner of the escape room the next town over. I designed rooms for him. Rather than wait for me to come up with something new, Fred suggested I just tweak the old designs of places I've done work for before. A medieval dungeon design became a 'top-secret prison' and that was it." He winced.

"Fred said he recycled designs from his other locations, not that he recycled your designs for other clients," I pointed out, not that I'd have expected him to admit the latter.

"Oh, he did—we did—both. The secret prison design is up and running in Platteville, that's how the other guy saw it. When he heard Fred was opening so close to his own escape room with the same design, well, that was it. He started hounding both Fred and me. Fred's so good at giving people he doesn't want to speak to the slip, though. I'm surprised he caught up to him."

So that was what the urgent calls had been about? The problem? This client being upset about the stolen designs?

"I should have never done it." Karter buried his face in his hands. "Now we're facing a lawsuit, and neither of us has the cash for a lawyer—and what's the point? I barely changed the designs. Why do I always let him talk me into cutting corners?"

With a jolt, I observed several things.

Karter kept talking about Fred as if he were still alive, and besides, he'd been out of town and wasn't paranormal as far as I could tell. I didn't think he'd had anything to do with his death.

But also… "Cutting corners." Where had I

heard that recently?

"You've done similar stuff for him before?" Roan asked.

Karter dropped his hands, a snarl on his face. "I don't see how that would be relevant." He frowned. "Do you... Do you think someone he cheated wanted him dead? Was it murder, not an accident? Did you tell me that piano nonsense because you suspect *me*?" Karter stood, and Roan slipped his notepad into his front pocket.

"Calm down, sir. You're not a suspect, and we don't think the man's death was anything but an accident." He shot me a look. We both knew that wasn't true.

"Please, take a seat at the dining table," said Javier soothingly. "You said you'd stay for dinner—"

"I don't think I can eat." Karter snatched his phone off the table. It didn't look turned on, so I hadn't even noticed it. I supposed if I were being hounded by angry clients and lawsuits, I'd shut my phone off, too.

"Wait!" Zashil called after him. I stood alongside him, tossing the faxed paper on the table. Zashil's eyes darted to it. "Who's going to own Beauchamp Entertainment Enterprises now?"

"I don't know." Karter bristled. "He hired me on a contract basis. I didn't franchise from him—I suppose the lawyers will have to figure out if the franchise operators can buy their locations outright or if his heirs will take over."

"Who are his heirs?" Roan asked.

"You'd have to ask his lawyer." Karter turned on his heel. "I told you, he has no family, so your guess is as good as mine." He took the few steps up to the hallway at a run and soon the door opened, followed by a rattling clatter, some incoherent muttering, and then the door slammed, as hard as if a gust of wind had shut it.

I blinked. "Broomie?"

I ran up the stairs and headed down the hallway.

My hat was no longer behind the door.

And more importantly, Broomhilde was no longer leaning near the umbrella stand.

"What?" I ignored all the cries asking me what was wrong and ripped open the door. The lock jammed a bit, like the vacuum suction of the door had broken some part in the door handle, and I steadied both hands over it, crying, "NEPO!"

But the door didn't open.

No.

"Let me through," said Arjun. "The door can stick sometimes if slammed."

I stepped back, my throat growing dry.

After what felt like forever, Arjun jostled it open.

On the other side was a bucket filled to the brim with red, glowing ectoplasm.

Para-paranormal.

And beside it, on the ground, was Karter's phone, its screen cracked—along with one shoe.

Chapter Seventeen

"What in the world...?" Roan stood beside me as everyone fanned out across the porch.

"Where did this come from?" asked Goldie.

I didn't have time to explain to her what it was. "The escape room," I said, remembering Draven had told me Cable had gathered it and stuck it in the backroom at the former bowling alley.

Zashil looked pale and Javier steadied him.

"What's it doing here?" Arjun asked.

"As pressing as that issue is, we might have a more pressing one." Roan pointed to the phone and the shoe, then to one of the cars in the driveway I hadn't recognized. "Where is Mr. Wattana?"

"Abducted." The word escaped my lips before I could explain how I knew. "And whoever did it knew to take Broomie, my hat—to make me powerless around the house with this bucket of para-paranormal."

"Para-para…?" asked Goldie. She'd been told the story of what had happened last month, but she hadn't been there.

"They're in trouble," was all I said. My heart wrenched at the thought of Broomie in danger, of another out-of-towner at risk. Broomie was bonded to die when I did, but she could die first without me following if she was broken apart into too many pieces. It had been known to happen, according to my mom, the witches left without broomsticks for all of their days.

"Who took them?" asked Zashil, his voice croaking.

"Whoever killed Fred," I said simply. "I have to believe Karter was the target—that Broomie and the hat and the para-paranormal was just to keep me from getting in the way."

"Does this mean Fred's death was related to his out-of-town troubles after all?" Roan asked. "Why else would whoever killed him care about Karter, too?"

"If they wanted Karter dead, why not kill him right here?" Arjun asked.

Why, indeed.

"Because Eithne likes to amuse herself," I muttered. A thought struck me. "The escape room!"

Zashil looked as if I'd slapped him. "Huh?"

"They took him there, I'm sure of it!" I gestured my hands out to either side of me. "Does anyone else have any ideas?"

"No," said Roan, picking Karter's phone and shoe up. "But I have to get back to the station. We might need to call in backup."

"To *Luna Lane?*" I asked.

Roan frowned. "If we can save this man—"

I chewed my lip. "Do what you have to. Meet us there." I spun on Zashil. "Drive me to the escape room?"

A series of footfalls against the hard concrete sidewalk drew my attention. "What's wrong?" Faine was scurrying up the walkway, Cable on her heels. "What's that smell…?" Her face blanched as she took in the bucket. "How did that get there?" She looked to Cable.

"I don't know." He gripped me by the arm and pulled me down the walkway. "But you should stand back from it."

Faine followed us both toward the driveway and I filled them in on the most pressing matters.

"Broomie?" Faine gasped.

"And you honestly think this man was taken to Spooky Escape Games?" Cable added.

"Where else?" I posited. "It's worth checking out."

Zashil and Javier were conferring, and Zashil followed after us, fishing a ring of keys out of his pocket. "I'll take you there."

Roan and Arjun were already halfway to the Mahajans' car, Roan probably having asked him for a lift to the station.

"Okay," I said, looking past him at Javier and Goldie grimly. Better they stayed behind.

We all filed into one of the unfamiliar cars, Zashil at the wheel, his headlights flicking on because the sun had set and the town was bathed in darkness.

In the second time in so many days, I took a wild and harried car ride through the streets of Luna Lane, speeding toward the site of my biggest mistake.

"WOLG," I said to my fingers, and they lit up, getting a quick glance from Zashil.

"Your powers work?" he asked.

"Looks like." I smiled weakly. It made sense since we were putting distance between me and that bucket, but I had to be sure.

Zashil took another harsh turn and gunned it down the road. I felt a little nauseous, and it may have just been the fact that I wasn't used to riding in cars or it may have been my nerves, but either way, I vowed to avoid riding in the things ever again if it could be helped.

The brakes squealed as Zashil parked smackdab in the street in front of the escape room. We all filed out of the car and Zashil ripped his keys out of the ignition, sorting through them with shaky hands as he approached the glass door.

He needn't have bothered. It opened slowly, the lights in the lobby flickering on as if to invite us.

"Hello?" Zashil called, stepping inside. I quickly pushed past him.

"Karter?" I called out. "Broomie?"

Cable and Faine filed in behind me, Faine tossing her purse on the nearest bench in the lobby.

There was a series of shouts from beyond the escape room door.

Jingling the keys again, Zashil went to unlock the door leading to the secret prison escape room, but it was unlocked.

"Hello?" I cried as I stepped inside.

A quick, rapid slamming against a set of iron bars caught my attention.

"Broomhilde!" I shouted, running to the left-most cell and gripping on to the bars.

Inside, Broomie leaned stiff against the back of the cell wall, lifeless. Beside her was…

"Draven?"

His hands clenched into fists at his side and he pointed to the coffin behind him that had never been in this room before. *His* coffin. "Who moved this here? What kind of joke is this? I woke up locked inside this room!" He squeezed his eyes shut tightly. "I've tried and I can't become chiropteran!"

"Chiro-what-ran?" asked Cable.

"He means 'a bat,'" I explained quickly.

"Me, neither!" cried Qarinah from another of the cells. Faine rushed over to peer inside and nodded, confirming that both our resident vampires had been kidnapped in their sleep, trapped inside these escape rooms.

I tugged on the cell door, but it wouldn't open. I waved my hands at it. "NEPO!" Nothing. How? Faine tried Qarinah's cell to the far right to no avail.

"Is this Karter?" Cable asked, pulling away from the iron-bar-covered window into the center jail cell. I rushed over and peeked inside. Karter was there, slumped over, one shoe off, unconscious—or already dead.

I swallowed. "Yes." I tried the door. Of course it wouldn't open.

"What is going on?" barked Draven.

If only I knew. If only I could put it all together.

"The control room," said Zashil sharply, and he left. I ran after him, rushing past the front desk to another unlocked door.

Inside, the computers were already booted up and Zashil slammed his keys on the desk beside one of the several monitors and started pressing buttons on the keyboard.

"No, no, no, not again," he said.

"Not again?" I leaned over his shoulder.

He clicked on the mouse and tried a few things,

but nothing happened. I looked to the monitor displaying the escape room from several angles—Draven and the unconscious Broomie in one cell, Qarinah alone in another, Karter's unconscious body in a third, while Cable and Faine coordinated together to try different things, pushing buttons and even trying to rip a fake, sci-fi-looking laser gun off the wall.

"This is what happened when the trap door fell on Fred and Jamie. The keys are stuck." He pointed to the keyboard and I noticed some were recessed.

"What does that mean?"

"I can't input the codes to unlock the doors." He shot up, sending his desk chair flying back. I had to jump out of the way as he crawled under the desk. "Maybe the connection's wrong—or there's another keyboard."

I turned to head back to my friends, then noticed the keys weren't pushed down in the keyboard anymore. "Try again!" I said.

Zashil crawled back up.

The keys got pressed down and locked in place before he could touch them.

"What's happening?" he asked, spinning on me.

"It wasn't me!" I held up my hands and spoke "LAEVER!" Reveal what, I didn't know.

But nothing happened.

"WOLG?" I tried desperately, looking at my fingertips.

Nothing again.

"Para-paranormal," I said. But that bucket was still back at the Mahajans'! How? Unless… "There was a bit left from last month that went down one of the bowling alley lanes."

Zashil's lips pinched together as he stared at me, but he didn't ask. "So now what?"

"I… I don't know."

With a clatter, something like papers falling in the lobby caught our attention.

We both ran out. Faine's purse was on the floor, its contents spread out. The copies of the blueprints.

Which wouldn't help at all right now.

But perhaps out of some instinct or for lack of anything actually useful to do just then, Zashil dashed forward and started stacking the scattered sheets.

"Zashil, leave those," I said. "We have to get those doors open—"

"This isn't right," said Zashil, staring at the top piece of paper in his hand.

My blood ran cold. "What do you mean?"

It was a diagram of one of the cells—the one with the trap door. I remembered examining it the closest on Roan's computer screen.

Zashil pointed to the top corner. There was a date and a location. "These are the original Creekdale designs." He flipped through them. "There isn't a single change since I last saw them—back in Creekdale. There were supposed to be changes."

"I thought Fred reused most of his designs."

And stole them from other people who were Karter's clients, apparently.

"Yes, but he said he had Karter updated the Luna Lane ones specifically. Now I have to wonder if it was to try to make the rooms different enough to avoid losing the copyright lawsuit." He grimaced.

That was troubling. "Do you honestly think Karter designed a deathly trap into the Luna Lane specs…? And Fred didn't notice?"

"Fred wasn't an architect. I doubt he would have."

Okay. But Karter would have had to have assumed any construction worker worth their salt would have pointed it out and refused to build it that way.

Except I wasn't worth my salt as a construction worker. And *I* had built it.

"Karter put a real trap door in the design as a joke?" I asked.

"Maybe." Zashil shrugged. "Maybe something to get his wayward friend's attention for once."

Well, he'd gotten his attention, all right.

"That still doesn't explain…" I gestured around me. This abduction. And Karter putting something in the design leading to Fred's death only made sense if there hadn't been para-paranormal. My magic alone—if it had indeed been unintentionally dark—shouldn't have resulted in the goo.

There had to be a second paranormal player— or two, if my magic hadn't been tainted at all.

Car brakes squealed outside.

Roan popped out of Arjun's vehicle as Arjun stayed inside to park the car in a better fashion along the curb, though with Zashil's car still out there in the middle of the road, it would make little difference.

"Did you call for help?" I asked Roan as he stepped inside, already short of breath.

"Not yet," he said, surprising me. "I updated Abdel and left the decision up to him—but, Lia, we have another problem. Autopsy came back on Fred. He was crushed *after* death. Cause of death was asphyxiation."

"*Asphyxiation*?" echoed Zashil.

"But how?" I said. "Fred was talking right before he was…" I snapped my mouth shut a moment. "Jamie did think maybe he was coughing —choking?"

"When?" Roan asked.

"As he was crawling through the trap door tunnel."

"That makes no sense," said Zashil. "I don't have a camera in the tunnel, but I didn't see anyone go in or out besides Jamie and Fred."

"Unless they were waiting inside the tunnel?" I proposed.

"How?" Roan asked, though he was simply asking, getting the facts. "When?"

"And where did they go afterward?" Zashil asked, stumbling over to the reception counter and slamming down the stack of blueprint copies he still carried. "I lost control over the trap doors, but after… After I heard the screams, they released, sliding back upward. No one got past any of us."

"Do you think there's an escape hatch that leads out the tunnel?" I asked.

"A secret trap door within a trap door?" Roan scratched his chin.

Just then, Qarinah's airy, singsong voice called out, shouting some kind of instructions to Faine and Cable, and Roan's relatively calm demeanor fled. His skin grew flush.

"Yeah, we have another problem—" I started, but Roan was already entering the open door to the escape room.

I ran after him, and just as I did, Arjun's voice trailing into the reception area from the sidewalk inside, the door behind me slammed shut with such force, the very walls shook. I stumbled into the open escape room doorway and spun around. Arjun on the outside, Zashil on the inside, attempted to open the door leading to the sidewalk. It wouldn't budge.

"What is going on?" Zashil slammed his fists against the glass door.

A peal of thunder growled out across the sky, and Faine whimpered.

"Eithne?" I murmured.

Then, with a strange, pushing force on my back, I stumbled into the escape room proper, the door leading to the lobby slamming shut, too.

The lights dimmed in the escape room, leaving only flickering overhead bulbs to illuminate our surroundings.

Roan's face glinted in the dim light, hovering as he was by the cell in which Qarinah was imprisoned.

"Lia, there was something else," he said, straightening and turning my way. His brow looked especially harrowed in the dim light. "The bruises indicated hands on the neck—long fingers, small, likely belonging to a child or a woman."

"A child or a woman…?" I asked. "Would a child have had the strength?"

Something caught in my throat, an impossible idea that nonetheless explained everything.

Gurgling sounds from the center cell caught our attention.

Cable was nearest. He peered inside. "He's choking!"

Karter?

"On what?" asked Faine.

I was at Cable's side in an instant, and he stepped back to let me peer inside. Karter was writhing on the floor, his hands weakly reaching up toward his own throat but far from touching it—yet *something* was keeping him pinned down, confining his movements to writhing on the floor.

"Virginia…?" The name escaped my lips softly at first, but when nothing changed, I had to put my theory to the test even harder. "Virginia!"

With a final gurgle, Karter fell limply to the ground.

Chapter Eighteen

A few moments passed, and the drip, drip, drip of something new caught my attention. Behind me on the wall, in the direction of the backroom, was the telltale trail of green ectoplasm that Virginia left behind when she went through solid surfaces.

A skill that would let her wait in a tunnel to choke a man—making her hands corporeal as necessary—and vanish out of sight.

The doors to the cells opened as one, and with a cry, Qarinah and Roan embraced, Cable thinking faster than I did and rushing inside the middle cell to check on Karter, Faine close behind him.

Cable's head popped up from Karter's face, his fingers on his neck. "He has a faint pulse—and he's breathing."

So Virginia hadn't finished the job?

Zashil's voice came from somewhere above us—speakers, I realized.

"I'm not doing this," said Zashil. "The keyboard is depressing on its own, the mouse moving…"

Virginia wasn't always visible, especially when there was a sample of para-paranormal in her vicinity. She'd been *holding down the keyboard keys* in person as Zashil had attempted to take control?

But she'd have had to have choked Fred really fast before zipping to the control room. Though that would explain the green stain on Jamie's mangled leg. A splash of her ectoplasm.

Draven walked out holding Broomhilde, his other hand on his hip, his expression stern. I took the broom from him and pet her, but she didn't respond. My heart sank. The para-paranormal was having an effect on her. The closer she'd gotten to it before, the less lifelike she'd become.

The doors to the middle and rightmost cells slammed shut again, trapping Cable and Faine with the unconscious Karter in the middle, Qarinah and Roan together in the rightmost cell.

Another voice came over the intercom—no, it hovered far closer.

"This is a fine selection of Games Club members," Virginia, still invisible to my eye, said. "You can thank me for transporting the vampire coffins here while they were sleeping so they could participate. So let's play. Fairly. No cheating—or I'll trap you here until it's been long enough so Karter Wattana can't get the help he needs."

My free hand shook in front of me. I had a feeling it'd fail, but I had to try. "LAEH," I said to see if I could somehow heal Karter through the bar window over the cell.

"You won't be able to use magic, Dahlia. I'd call that cheating, for one—but I've hidden the last bit of para-paranormal Ravana sent shooting down the bowling alley lane somewhere in this room, somewhere where it seems to have affected you."

I gritted my teeth. "Your actions created far more of the stuff."

"Yes, I know. I brought the bucket of it to the Mahajans' so I could kidnap Karter from under your nose." There was a coldness to her voice. "But I *did* find that first sample in the flask when I explored the bowling lane that day you enchanted yourself an escape room. Eithne had tasked me with searching for it."

"Eithne? You worked with her, then? Why?" Draven shouted out from beside me.

"I don't have to explain myself to you!" Virginia answered. "Now get in the third cell and let the game begin—or do you not want a chance of saving that wretched man Fred *still* managed to talk into cutting corners?"

Cutting corners. There was that phrase again. A form of cheating, to be sure, which would at least partially explain why it bothered her. But why was she so unreasonable, so inflexible about cheating at all?

I supposed I was about to find out.

I stepped inside the open cell door, Broomie in my grip.

"Really?" asked Draven dryly. "You do remember this is the cell with the lethal trap door?"

"You can turn into a bat and fly, can't you?" I bit my tongue. No, he couldn't. He'd told me so.

Draven wrinkled his nose. "That dreadful stuff. I can't change, remember?"

"No cheating!" repeated Virginia.

Sighing, Draven stepped inside, examining his hand, front to back. In the dim light, I wasn't sure what he was noticing. Perhaps he was just trying to imagine it as a bat wing.

The door slammed shut behind him.

"Do I need to even check to see that it's locked again?" he said, almost bored. He stuffed his hand under his elbow as he crossed his arms.

I shook my head.

"Excellent," said Virginia's disembodied voice. "Zashil? Please begin. But know that I'll be watching. No funny business."

Zashil's voice quavered, but he spoke, sounding as if reading through a script without enthusiasm. "You have been unfairly imprisoned by a shadowy force, along with your group of friends."

Tell me about it.

"You will be executed at dawn without trial," he

continued. "Fortunately, someone from your group, the *team name*—"

"Spooky Games Club," said Virginia, a hint of her bright, cheery demeanor shining through. Glad *she* thought this was all a game.

"From the Spooky Games Club," Zashil continued, undaunted, "has caused a distraction outside, leading the prison guards away. Unfortunately, they can only keep their attention for one hour. Escape before then, using clues left behind by other successful escapees before you, or face immediate execution upon the guards' return. Time begins… Now."

With a rumble of recorded thunder and a flash of a strobe light likely intended to mimic lightning, a tick, tock sound rung out overhead. Through the little grated window in the cell door, I could see four numbers on the opposite wall quickly counting down: 59:48.

"What do we do now?" Qarinah's voice echoed loudly throughout the room.

Broomie's lovely white scrap fabric ribbon brushed against my bare leg, unwinding and jangling out to me as if she were conscious and handing it my way. But there was no movement from her.

"We search the cells," I called out loudly, setting Broomie back against the wall. I untied the ribbon around her and held it between my lips. "And find some clues." My long hair gathered at the back of my head, I tied it back with the ribbon, ready to get to work.

Qarinah and Roan began describing anything that seemed out of place in their cell, and Faine and Cable joined in, too. I wondered if they remembered Jamie's story, that the center and rightmost cells got unlocked before the one Draven and I were in, but I was afraid to shout it out, afraid Virginia would take it as cheating and keep us all locked in the game until it was too late. Too late for Karter. Maybe too late for any of us.

"She's an awful strong ghost, if she was able to carry our coffins in here." Draven walked around the cell, looking at the walls but offering no help when it came to finding any clues. I noticed I'd leaned Broomie against a word puzzle carved in the form of a message, so I shifted her to get a closer look.

"She carried Karter here, too," I said quietly, reading the message. Cable and Qarinah were communicating some kind of code they each had the piece of to one another, Roan attempting to input their guesses into a lock hidden on his cell door's hinges.

"The para-paranormal doesn't affect her paranormal abilities?" Draven asked. His voice was quiet, like he only wanted *me* to hear him.

"She's dead," I said. "The most it could do is erase her, I'd guess—which it kind of does by making her invisible."

"Which she could surely choose to be at any point," he said. "Without this substance around, does she stay visible at all times, it just being a matter of whether or not there's someone around to see her?"

"I… I hadn't thought about it," I said, pretending to inspect the riddle closer. Roan and Qarinah let out a little cry of delight and it sounded like their cell door swung open.

"She stayed invisible for eight or nine decades. At least she did for the four or so I was here since her demise."

"What do you mean?" I asked.

Faine's voice traveled closer. "Dahlia? Draven? What do you have? We're looking for an eight-letter word on a lock outside our door."

"Or a pattern of colors," added Qarinah from out in the "guards'" area.

"Or a series of numbers," added Roan. "There are a lot of puzzles to solve out here."

"I might have some of the letters." I read the scrawled message out loud, sure to emphasize the four letters I'd just noticed were drawn backward. "'Might you seek escape, unite your efforts and remain calm. Don't despair.' M. U. R. D."

I was so used to speaking backward for my spells, it really had taken an extra moment to notice —besides, it was subtle with the "M" and the "U," just a flourish at the upper right of each letter that appeared backward.

"Maybe that goes with the message we have scrawled on the wall in here," said Cable. "'Engage your brain and read deeper to reveal the truth.' Two 'e's and two 'r's are upside down."

M.U.R.D.E.R.E.R. Murderer. Well, that wasn't grim at all. It also didn't fit the high-tech prison theme of the room. Shouldn't it have?

Wasn't this the puzzle Fred had insisted had been incorrect?

"That's it!" said Roan excitedly, and with another click, the center door opened.

We were as far as the first group had gotten before it had all gone wrong.

"Fifty-two minutes," shouted Cable as he moved into the guards' area. And we were moving far faster than that first group was.

Almost time for the trap door that could squash us flat.

Draven crouched beside me, seeming to inspect the scrawled message, though it was likely no longer in play. "*You* were here for a while before the ghost showed herself. I suppose you would have been a child… I don't remember. I didn't interact with you much before you came of age."

I sat back against the wall, my bottom hitting the cold black and white floor tiles.

I thought hard. Virginia…

"Hello, little witch."

Faine and I were sneaking in the bushes at the edge of the woods, about to scare Hitesh and Zashil, who were playing battling wizards somewhere up ahead. They hadn't invited us —the actual witch who could throw down some enchantments —so I'd suggested we sneak up on them and scare them with an enchantment. Maybe a shower of frogs or something. Not that I'd ever attempted such an enchantment before. I might have had to settle with making my hands glow and shouting at them.

Faine yelped, more like a dog than a human, and cowered behind me, snatching Broomie out of the air and gripping on to her shaft for dear life, as if she'd clobber whoever had spoken with my broomstick companion. Broomhilde stiffened and snapped to it, puffing up and stretching her bristles to seem bigger, allowing my best friend to wield her.

"Little pup, I won't hurt you," said the airy, chilling voice.

I whipped around, my too-big witch's hat falling down over my face, even as I held my arms out and tried to seem threatening.

"Who are you?" I asked, but I couldn't see at all.

"Just a friendly ghost," said the woman.

I shifted my hat up to peek a little under the brim.

The woman was beautiful—and inhumanly pale. Paler even than the vampires.

She looked like someone who'd stepped out of a historical movie—long skirt, puffy-shouldered blouse that clasped at her neck with a plain gold brooch, along with a parasol and bonnet.

"Where did you come from?" I barked, offering Faine a reassuring pat behind me. Broomie gave off a little bee-like hum, as if to tell me she had our backs.

Somewhere off in the woods, the brothers were laughing, casting play spells with Latin words, as if that would be enough to harness magical energy into enchantments. Mom had told me the Poplar motto in the potions book was in Latin because that was what our ancestors had once spoken. But even they'd had to speak their native tongue backward for enchantments to take effect.

The woman smiled. It was dazzling. "I'm Virginia Kincaid, little witch. I just wanted to welcome you to the neighborhood."

"I'm not little!" I protested. "And I've been here ten whole years!"

"Hmm, so you have." She fluffed her washed-out pale, yellow hair. "Ten years old and so feisty. And I'm, I suppose, to be forever twenty-one."

In the hand not clutching her parasol, something else washed-out appeared out of thin air—a book.

She flipped through it. "Yes. Yes… A simpler time. Tragic, to be sure, but it makes for a more passionate story." *She flipped the book closed. I read the title slowly.* The Sound and the Fury. *I wondered what kinds of sounds made someone so angry. "I died with this book in my hands," she said quietly. "Don't you think it makes for a more romantic afterlife?" She stuck her hands out and twirled, the book disappearing. Her eyes shone red for just a moment, and she began laughing, light and airy.*

"Dahlia," Faine whispered in my ear as she tugged on my sleeve. "She's scary." Broomie shifted her brush head to rub up against Faine's cheek.

But I wasn't scared of anything. At least—I was determined not to be.

My knees wobbled just a little, though. And it would take several more meetings with the elegant ghost lady before they stopped shaking entirely.

I blinked, coming out of my memory. That had been our first introduction—and I'd been ten?

And she'd…

I didn't see how I hadn't realized it before, she'd said as much then. She'd modeled her look after her novel.

That didn't mean she'd actually died a hundred years before.

Chapter Nineteen

*T*he shouts ringing out throughout the rest of the room, as other members of the club ran around, back into the cells and outside of them, filtered out through my brain as I sat there in silence, thinking about it.

Draven slid down beside me, hugging his knees to his chest. "You figured something out?" he asked quietly, then louder, he said, "A flaw in the design, no? Nothing much for us to do in this cell while everyone else is solving puzzles out there."

That seemed to satisfy Virginia. Perhaps she was keeping a closer eye on our teammates, making sure they solved each puzzle without cutting corners or otherwise cheating.

"Colors! Over here, here!" shouted Qarinah. She'd spotted some possible solution.

"She died when I was ten," I said quietly, my hand reaching for Broomie's shaft for something to anchor myself with. "Not the turn of the twentieth century. The turn of the twenty-first."

"Twenty years ago?" Draven scratched his cheek. The light was still so dim in here, but there was something off about his hand. "Sounds right," he said.

I snatched his hand in mine. It was… Just the slightest bit cold, like an ice pack left out to acclimate to room temperature. The skin didn't feel as smooth and marble-like as it once had.

"You're changing…?" I whispered harshly.

Draven cracked a sad half-smile and I saw one of his incisors was about half the length. "Maybe prolonged exposure to that para-paranormal. Who knows how long our coffins have been sitting here, near the vial of foul stuff she's stored away."

My heart clenched. "I'm sorry I asked you to take it away last time. I put you in danger—"

He put a single, slightly warm finger to my lips. "We didn't know. Let's get through this and out of here—our time is short, but we're already working against the clock in more ways than one. No need to panic anyone any further."

Clenching my teeth, I threaded my fingers through the hair at the top of my scalp. How could Virginia do this? She was *our friend*. Annoying at times, sure, but she'd saved my life just last month…

"So if she died twenty years ago," said Draven quietly, "suffice it to say the story about her burning to death in a house located right here couldn't be true. The bowling alley has been here since the fifties."

There was that, too.

Faine let out a groan as some kind of error beep rang out. They'd inputted the wrong code for something.

"Try red, blue, green, yellow!" shouted Cable.

It dawned on me, then. "But do you know what *could* be true? She could have known these two— Fred and Karter." My toes tapped the floor, restless. "They'd have to be in their forties or early fifties, if I had to guess."

"So in their twenties most likely when our dear local specter actually passed away?"

There was another error sound for a lock not working and this time, it was Faine who shouted out a pattern of colors. Thank goodness they were keeping their heads in the game. Time was running out—for Karter, for Draven and Qarinah, perhaps. Maybe for all of us.

"It would be a strange coincidence," added Draven.

"Would it, though? Karter said they both grew up in Creekdale. And Fred admitted to 'spending time in Creekdale.' He said he'd even heard the rumors about Luna Lane. He'd just laughed them off."

"So they were our neighbors? What does that have to do with Virginia haunting us?"

Shifting, I leaned on one thigh. "Eithne used to live in the woods."

"Not since your mother moved in," he said.

It was strange to be speaking of this so casually with him now, not feeling even a shred of anger at him for keeping this information from me.

"Not as far as any of you *knew*. But she was around—she cursed me, she killed my mom. She's probably been watching me most of my life, enjoying the way her curse makes me scrub and dust and ache like Cinderella."

"So… What? Virginia's from Creekdale, she died there, and Eithne made her a ghost haunting Luna Lane?"

"Well, she couldn't haunt Creekdale. There are no paranormal people there."

"And she had a grudge against Fred and this… Karter?"

"*Something* had to have made it possible for her to linger as a ghost. Some kind of regret. A witch could trap a soul in an object, as we've seen, if so inclined, but she can't let her wander around a town unless she herself actually isn't ready to cross to the realm beyond."

Draven pursed his lips. "These are theories?"

"No, I… I just know it to be true. I summon my mom every so often—we've talked about Virginia, what it means to be a ghost left behind." I caressed the scale on the back of my hand. "How I thought Mom might have some regret, leaving me to deal with this curse on my own. But she said, as much as she hated leaving me, it wasn't the same. Something *strong* has to linger in a soul's spirit to leave them behind like that. Usually something darker. Something like the hope of revenge."

"I thought it was always regret at not marrying her 'betrothed,'" he said, mocking Virginia's haughty way of speech on the last word.

"We got it!" shouted Roan from outside our door. A light flashed green and he slammed against something with a click. A button perhaps. That ostensibly opened a trap door.

Only it took a few seconds more for the grinding, groaning chains to begin pulling up the door.

Because Zashil was actually controlling it. And Zashil would hesitate to open it up, all things considering—even if it *was* our only method of escape.

I stared at the rising trap door, the creaking, chain-recoiling sounds sending chills down my spine. Zip through. Virginia didn't have a grudge against either of us, surely?

Green ectoplasm streaked down the wall, dripping over the open trap door.

"Virginia?" I asked, but I couldn't see her.

Her voice rang out in the air. "It was both," she said, as if she'd been listening to us all along. "Revenge and anger that I never married—even if I hated my fiancé with every fiber of my being by then."

Flickering, almost so translucent she wasn't there, she appeared before us.

She took her historical bonnet off and her long hair came tumbling down. Shimmering, out of focus, her turn-of-the-twentieth-century attire became something out of another turn-of-the-century entirely.

A spaghetti strap tank top, three-quarters khakis with a long chain dangling out of her hip pocket.

"You're right," she said. "I died twenty years ago just outside of Creekdale, not Luna Lane. Eithne took hold of my spirit wandering the woods and offered me a chance to begin a new life in the afterlife. A chance for…"

"Revenge?" I posited.

"What's going on?" Cable's head poked through the little bars lending a view inside. "Are you afraid to go through?"

"We need you to finish this game," Faine called. Her voice echoed down the tunnel on the other side of the trap door, waiting just beyond to welcome us to safety.

But in front of the trap door floated this more contemporary Virginia, her eyes blazing red.

"Fred asked me to marry him, and then he cheated on me," she said, her voice growing dark and gravelly. "And then he—and his simpering friend—killed me."

Chapter Twenty

*V*irginia had been murdered—and in my lifetime.

Suddenly, so much made sense. Her anger around Spindra making out with her former fiancé —the man who'd killed her. The stealthy appearance of the second paranormal presence responsible for the new para-paranormal after Fred's death.

"Dahlia?" called Faine from down the tunnel.

"Everyone, stay right where you are!" I said. No sense in anyone else getting within range of Virginia right now. Her eyes shone red, brighter than any vampire's, more twisted with hate.

"What do you mean, they killed you?" I asked.

Her nostrils flared. "There was an accident. He was always going on about how he'd make so much money. We were fresh out of college and he'd invested everything he had into this idea he and his classmate had: prefab sheds."

"Sheds," I hissed, remembering the word had come up before—right before Fred's death, according to Jamie.

"They built their first one in the woods between Creekdale and Luna Lane," she said. "He was so proud of himself—got some company that, '*nudge, nudge, worked for less*.'" Though her voice was high-pitched, shrill, she imitated Fred's cadence perfectly. "He didn't need permits or any other hassle to have a prototype built in the woods, he said. No one ever came out that way. They'd figure out how to transport it in a truck once they got their first client."

I didn't like how this was going at all.

"I was stupid and in love," she continued. In her hands appeared that worn paperback and she clutched it to her chest. "The long absences, the late hours—I never questioned any of it. He was a busy man with dreams. Of course he was occupied so much of the time. I loved stories—romances, tragedies—and when Fred started flirting with me one day at a party, he swept me off my feet." Her dreamy expression narrowed. "Little did I know, he attempted to sweep just about any woman he encountered off her feet—and succeeded at least a fraction of the time."

I wanted to offer her reassurances, but I didn't know what to say.

"But he asked *me* to marry him." Ginny's irises glowed brighter now. The tick, tick, tock of the escape room clock counting down outside our cell continued in the background. "I know now it was because my dad had money." She laughed darkly. "Seems like something right out of these period romances. The suitor targeting a woman for her dowry, or in my case, a trust fund—a fund I never sought, nor needed, as long as I had love. But he robbed me of my chance to collect either way."

"What happened?" I croaked.

"He invited me to see the first shed they'd had built—*bragged* about instructing Karter to cut corners, make it as cheap as possible, how he'd been hard to convince but had broken in time, as the sniveling creature still seems wont do to." She focused her anger on the wall behind me leading to the center cell before turning back to me. I froze, my hand just reaching for the bottom of Broomie's shaft. I was going to *speed crawl* through that tunnel if need be and I was taking her with me. I didn't know what Virginia had in store for any of us, in her state.

"It was dark, so he carried an oil lantern for light, which made the ambiance seem all rustic and romantic. He knew I was a sucker for those old-fashioned kinds of things. The shed was two stories, the second story being a loft. I was impressed at first. Looked cozy, like something out of a farm, there in the middle of the woods. We were just enjoying the quiet at first. We talked and then I read while Fred called Karter on his phone." She *had* been alive in the time of cellphones, even though I imagined they'd been of the primitive variety. Virginia fluffed at her hair. "Eventually, we were *stealing kisses* in the loft. When his phone rang again.

"He ignored it," she continued. "But it kept ringing and ringing. Finally, laughing, I yanked it out of his pocket and answered for him, though his face grew red and he tried to snatch it away." Her voice grew lower. "It was a woman, as confused to hear me answering as I was to hear her calling. We didn't talk for long, but we both managed to communicate that we considered ourselves Fred's fiancée.

"Fred screamed and slapped the phone out of my hand, breaking it. I pushed him, and he pushed me back. We fought." She bit her lip. "My head slammed against a beam and then the whole thing collapsed." She coughed and a spray of dust escaped from between her lips. A trickle of phantom blood ran down from her temple to her cheek, her hair mussed up, the book clutched to her chest. Her leg looked crushed then, bent awkwardly as it hung down. "I survived—we both did—the support fell just right and shielded us from much of the debris. The lantern even managed to fall without shattering."

Draven put a hand on my shoulder. A warm hand. I looked over and the faintest of wrinkles were forming on his features.

"A car pulled up," said Virginia, oblivious to anyone else's suffering just then. "It was Karter, come to check out the shed on Fred's invitation. I thought we were saved. Fred had a gash on his arm, and my leg, my head…" She paused to show us her grizzly wounds. "But I was still so angry with him. I shouted at him, for cutting corners on the building, for cheating on me—and then his hands, they… They…" She gripped her own throat, the book vanishing. "They wrapped around my neck and choked the life out of me."

My stomach roiled. Was that why she'd chosen to choke him back?

"Karter tried to pry him off me at first, but Fred pushed him away. And then… Karter just stopped fighting him. As he always does. Puts up a feeble protest, then just lets Fred cheat and cut corners and…" She gasped, letting out a choked cry.

"They burned the shed together, smashing the lantern to kindle the wood. I was found in the remains, but Fred managed to escape suspicion… somehow. Smooth-talked his way out of it, had his fiancée—his *other* fiancée—vouch for his where-abouts, claim I'd been out of my mind to ever tell my friends and family we'd been together. The contractors he'd worked with had been off the books. No one knew who'd built the burnt shed in the woods." Her voice grew soft. "I wandered the woods in despair. No one at home saw me, so I gave up wandering the streets of Creekdale. Eithne… She was the first person to talk back to me as I passed her by in the woods. She cried out to me from a tree branch and told me everything I'd ever heard about Luna Lane was true. She promised me I could have my revenge one day. All I had to do was keep an eye on you."

"Me?" I asked, taken aback.

She nodded. "'The little red-haired witch named Dahlia,'" she repeated.

"Why?" I asked.

She shrugged. "I never asked. Besides, you were never in danger here growing up, outside of your curse. I grew bored just watching over you and started blending in with the whole town. I almost forgot about it all, really, so happy was I to be Miss Kincaid, a woman I'd never truly been, a woman out of a romantic historical story."

Draven coughed. He actually *coughed* beside me, and when he pulled his hand back, it was covered in blood. He wasn't supposed to *have* blood. Outside in the guards' area, Qarinah began coughing too, Roan's muffled voice asking her what was the matter.

"Virginia!" I said quickly. "We need to get the vampires away from this place! They're… They're becoming human. Aging." I squeezed Draven's hand. It was far too warm.

Virginia's eyes widened as she seemed to take in Draven for the first time.

"I never meant—I never meant to hurt anyone else."

Draven chuckled, his voice throaty. "I'm sure Jamie appreciates those sentiments."

She scowled. "I got a little excited, my revenge so near at hand. I thought he was clear of it before I grabbed for Fred's throat."

Draven coughed again, and Faine whined like a dog from down the tunnel. "Virginia!" I cried.

"Ginny," she said, tucking a strand of hair behind her ear. "It was always just 'Ginny.'"

I scowled at her.

"Go through," she said, floating away from the trap door. "I won't let it fall on you."

I didn't hesitate. Encouraging Draven to go ahead of me, I picked up Broomie and crawled through on hands and knees, Draven's coughs echoing out in front of me, the clack of Broomie slamming against the hard floor, scraping against the stone above us that never should have been there, filling me with dread.

I tried not to look up, but I saw that though I was sure Cable had done his best, the stone was still smeared with a red glow, the essence of para-para-normal having sunk into its porous surface.

Perhaps Virginia had given us all a greater dose of the stuff than she'd intended for this long.

The speakers rumbled with fake thunder as Faine helped me to my feet. We were both clear of the cell, no crushing trap door. We ran out to join the others in the guards' area, Draven stumbling and Faine offering him her shoulder.

I stared down at Broomie in my hand. She still wasn't moving.

Qarinah sat in a chair in the corner that was probably meant to be a pretend guard's, Roan kneeling at her side.

"Virginia, open the door!" I said.

She floated through the closed cell door, green ectoplasm trailing behind her in her wake.

I stared her down. "Tell Zashil he can cancel the game."

The clock ticked down. We still had half an hour, but I was done with this. From the battered and forlorn looks of those around me, we all were.

"I can't," she said softly.

"You *can't?*" I repeated.

"He can't, either." She sighed. As if she needed to sigh. "The night I saw Fred again in Spindra's shop, doing what Fred did so very well"—her voice was tight at that—"I panicked and fled. I wandered the woods, and Eithne was waiting for me at that place we explored together, where you figured out her cabin had once been."

"In the flesh?" I asked. It came out as more of a gasp than I'd expected.

She nodded. "The witch reminded me of the revenge she'd promised me, assured me she had a plan to get Karter in town too—which started with retrieving that para-paranormal waiting in a flask under the bowling alley lane and taking it away so you could complete your enchantment without impediment." How thoughtful of *Eithne* to remember what I hadn't thought much of at the time. "And then, she swore to me, Fred would shortly fall victim to his own hubris. She insisted Karter would follow, after arriving in town to look for him." Virginia—Ginny—frowned. "I… I hesitated. I remembered how I felt when I thought Fred and I had been in love." She looked at her own hands now, though they were getting more and more difficult to see. "She told me what we could do, said the designs you were going to be working from were all wrong, that she hadn't even tampered with them. It was Karter's own weak form of revenge, she said, but that was so deliciously appropriate."

"The designs… included the death trap?" I asked.

"The designs you used on Fred's phone did."

Eithne had known this? Had she really cared that much about a promise she'd made to a ghost decades ago?

"She cast an enchantment as soon as you walked away after building it," Ginny said. "She was waiting for me after that in the back, in all that empty space set aside for another room. I just had to swing around the back of the building after hiding the para-paranormal down the block and phase through the wall."

"Ginny, please get to the point," snapped Draven, cradling his head. His hair was fair, so it was hard to tell, but I swore strands of gray were weaving throughout his locks.

Ginny scowled. "The enchantment, not me, is what pushes the buttons or stops Zashil from being able to take control of it. It's true that I lingered in the stone in the trap door tunnel, waited for Jamie to pass by, and then choked Fred, but then I flew off and did as Eithne instructed me, shouting for her, for her enchantment, whatever it was, to slam the stone down on Fred's head."

"So you weren't in the backroom, pressing down keys on the keyboard?" I asked. The enchantment was an active one, pressing keys and fighting Zashil from taking control whenever things went beyond the predetermined script?

"I wouldn't have been able to get there so shortly after choking him. Not without Eithne's teleportation magic."

"Teleportation magic?" This was very bad news.

Ginny clutched her elbow. "She teleported the vampires' coffins here for me, and also teleported Karter and me here once I grabbed him."

"I take it the para-paranormal doesn't affect *her* somehow?" Cable asked. He slipped in front of me slightly, as if offering to throw himself between Ginny and me if necessary.

"No." Ginny shook her head. "Not at all. Since it's her magic that sparks the creation of it, she's immune to it, she explained. Unless the substance was made by another witch, but I can't picture

Dahlia ever having a hand in such a monstrous creation."

That made one of us. Here I'd thought I'd had an unintentional role in it.

"Why?" I asked. "I know why you took Karter, but why bring the vampires here?"

Tears, if she could really cry, were pricking the corners of Ginny's eyes. "I just… I wanted to play with the Spooky Games Club one last time."

"As you murdered a man and put your friends in danger?" spat Roan. He didn't usually get angry, but he was shaking as he stood. Qarinah's head bobbed. She wasn't growing too old—she was a relatively new vampire—but she seemed depleted of energy.

Ginny nodded. "Once the deed was done, our prearranged plan continued. Eithne, or her enchantment, I didn't see her again after the day before the incident, teleported me to Spindra's shop so no one would suspect me. I asked to go there because I… I foolishly wanted to give her a piece of my mind for making out with my fiancé, even if most of me hated him." She wrung her hands together. "Even though I knew, maybe, it was just in Spindra's nature to go after him. Maybe she just wanted to devour him. Broomie…" She reached a ghostly hand toward my lifeless broom and I yanked my pet away from her. "She spotted me from the window outside just as I teleported into Spindra's shop, moments before Spindra herself stepped into it. I didn't know why Broomie followed me at first"—I did, it was Broomie trying to commiserate with her after being snubbed by me, in her eyes —"but then after everyone panicked and headed toward the escape room, I headed for the vampires' manor."

"Why?" Draven coughed and leaned against a wall, clinging desperately to something with no purchase.

"I wanted you in the escape room for the final game. Whenever Karter was coming, I wanted you to be ready, to make sure Eithne had done as I'd asked—"

"But Karter didn't arrive until the next day," I said.

"And the commotion in the escape room that day would have made the discovery of the vampires quick regardless. I wasn't thinking. But Eithne must have been. She waited until the next day to teleport them as we'd agreed, probably knew Karter was on his way and the game could begin at sunset."

"Broomie followed you to Draven's basement?" I asked.

"She startled me, but yes. I told her I was checking on them, and then when the coffins creaked, the lids sliding off, I just took off. I wasn't in the right frame of mind to keep lying. Not to someone as harsh as Draven, who might see right through me."

Draven cackled darkly. "I'm seeing right through you right now. In so many so interesting ways." His voice broke into coughs and Faine moved in to help him. I found my feet shifting to take his other side, handing Broomie off to Cable, who cradled her gingerly.

"Okay, Ginny. That's enough. Get us out of here!" I said.

"I can't!" she croaked again, putting her hands on her hips indignantly. "Eithne enchanted the room—we figured the business would close after my revenge was complete."

"We know she enchanted—" started Roan.

But Ginny cut him off. "For each and every game played. Zashil won't get control over it again until someone inside this room dies."

Chapter Twenty-One

The room broke out into a commotion of cries and shouting.

"Ginny, you'd… you'd kill one of us?" Faine asked.

Ginny pressed her palms over her cheeks, her shoulders slouching. Then she gestured behind us to the open center cell. "I assumed it would be Karter who died, of course! But that's why I didn't quite choke the life out of him. I thought he'd die after the game began. And then I'd still have one last game with you all—"

"You weren't even playing with us!" I shouted.

"I was!" She wrung her hands. "You just couldn't see me. The para-paranormal… I'm trying really, really hard right now for you to see me at all, and I'm still rather faded." She looked at her arms.

Draven brushed out of our grip and stumbled toward the center cell. "Out of my way," he said to

Cable, who stepped in front of him. "Given the circumstances, I think Abdel can excuse me sucking the last bit of life out of the man."

"*Draven!*" I shouted.

"No," said Roan. "If you murder someone in Luna Lane—"

"It'd be a mercy kill at this point," said Draven stubbornly. He tried to cross his arms but wavered on unsteady feet.

"Not if we can get him out of here," I said. "I can heal him."

Draven growled. "It's either him or Qarinah and me at this point—probably me first, that might do it. But I suppose there's nothing *illegal* about me sacrificing my own life for this? Just taking the life of the cheating, murdering human brat who wandered into town?"

The tick, tick, tock of the clock made me look at it. We were down to twenty minutes.

"Let's solve the room," I said.

Everyone turned to stare at me, even Ginny.

"Something to distract me before I die?" Draven laughed darkly and slumped to the ground, his back against the open center cell door. He looked over at Karter but didn't seem to have the heart—or maybe just the energy at this point—to end him.

I was risking a lot on this. Draven was right. He and Qarinah were not doing well. And if I had to choose—of course I'd rather save Draven, even if Karter had spent way fewer years on this planet.

But none of us were murderers. Well, none of us but Ginny, and she'd only become one out of desperation and after some twisted cajoling from Eithne Allaway.

"I… I just have a feeling," I said.

"A feeling?" Cable frowned.

"Eithne… She likes to be entertained. Maybe a scramble for our very lives—or at least the life of one of us—maybe that's more entertaining than one of us just ending it prematurely. Maybe she wove a way out of this in the enchantment itself—someone dies or we solve the game."

"Sure," said Draven darkly. "Why not? What other ideas do any of us have?"

Roan let out a sigh. "Zashil?"

"I'm still here." Zashil's voice was shaky over the intercom. "You have a few more puzzles—"

"Don't tell us!" I shouted. "Just in case… In case Ginny's hatred of cheating is a condition of the game." I locked eyes with the ghost. She smiled weakly.

I took Broomie from Cable's extended hand.

"All right," he said. "Let's do this."

Faine and Cable scrambled to show me the last three puzzles they'd identified in the room that they hadn't solved yet. One, a safe on the floor between the first two jail cells, was locked with a series of numbers. The other was a desk drawer—that just needed a key, though there were some lines scratched into the outside of the drawer. The final puzzle was a five-letter sequence that unlocked the final door to freedom.

"Let's start with the safe," I said, pinpointing it to be the next solvable puzzle. "Any hints about numbers?"

Faine and Cable scrambled around the room and I clutched Broomie tightly, the tip of her broom dragging over the floor as I did a saunter around the room myself. Qarinah and Draven were too weak to move and Roan crouched by Qarinah's side, the hard floor probably doing a number on his knees.

"She's clearing the way." Draven coughed and pointed a weak, gnarled finger. "Clearing the dust."

I looked down. There was a pile of dust around the guard's desk, and I was dragging Broomhilde across it.

Dust in a brand new escape room? There was a strange, unnatural streak of it leading outward.

Jamie's words about things having to be reset for each group, like kitty litter and sand and dust…

Borrowing Broomie for what she might at first glance have been intended for, I quickly brushed the dust away. "It's a math problem."

Cable rushed over. "I'm a humanities major, but I still got straight As," he offered. Of course he had. He crouched down and read the math, solving it in his head, apparently. Faine was already running to the safe. "Try 8-14-77," he said simply.

Ginny, so faded as to almost be invisible again, let out a startled cry.

The safe opened with a click. "It worked!" Faine put a hand inside and fumbled out a keyring full of about twenty keys.

"The desk!" I said.

She ran there and started trying keys in the drawer.

"Ginny?" I asked to the almost-translucent specter. "What did those numbers mean to you?"

The rattling of the keys as Faine and Cable kept trying the drawer echoed along with the tick, tick, tock of the timer, counting down now. Fewer than eight minutes until the end.

"My birthday," said Virginia weakly.

A 70s baby, huh? No wonder her references skewed a touch too modern. "I didn't know Fred even knew it."

"Could be a coincidence," Draven offered, entirely unhelpfully.

"I doubt that," I said. I jutted my chin toward Karter's unconscious form. At least the fact that we were still in this game meant that he wasn't yet dead. "He designed this room. My theory is he put real traps in here—maybe messages, too—to get Fred to slow down and take note. Only they were supposed to be discovered before or during construction—and Fred never took a closer look."

Ginny steepled her fingers in front of her mouth. "Was he trying to remind Fred of me?"

"If Fred remembered your birthday and could

recognize the significance," I offered. "I wonder how Karter even knew."

Ginny looked crestfallen.

"Got it!" said Faine with a flourish of the keys after what felt like forever. The drawer opened and she and Cable tackled the contents, pulling out scores of papers.

I ran over to help, leaning Broomie against the desk. We'd never have time to sort through it all. It was all full of important-looking jail paperwork. The clock above us displayed about four minutes now.

Faine whimpered, pulling her hand back quickly and wrinkling her nose.

"Dahlia," said Cable quietly. He gently extricated a small, familiar flask and held it above his head with two hands.

The original para-paranormal Ravana had left behind. Only a small bit glowed red at the bottom of the flask.

"Yeah. That's where I put it before we started today…" Ginny admitted sheepishly.

"Thanks for the warning," I snapped. "That's not all of it. There's more left behind in the tunnel."

Cable's face fell.

"You didn't know," I told him. "Just… Just put that in the corner."

I didn't know if that would help, but what else could we do at that point?

Faine was still shuffling inside the drawer, the

nausea she pushed through from the para-paranormal's lingering presence evident on her face.

"The drawer," Qarinah offered helpfully from where she sat across the room. Her voice cracked. "Remember the scratching on the drawer?"

Faine, Cable, and I looked at one another and scooped out the rest of the drawer's contents, which also included a healthy supply of office supplies and a tin of mints.

"There are more scratches inside." I pointed to them.

Cable traced a finger from the lines inside as they continued along the side of the drawer and to the front. "They're letters," he said. "See? This is a 'Y.'"

"The letter code for the final door!" said Faine, practically bouncing on her heels. For a moment, it was like she'd forgotten the stakes of our Games Club meeting here entirely.

"'N,'" I pointed out.

"An 'I,'" said Faine.

"Another 'N'?" said Cable aloud.

"'G,'" added Ginny quietly.

"Ginny?" I said back.

Right. The answer to the code. The clock was down to fifty-four seconds.

I sprinted across the room and turned the dial on the lock until it spelled "G-I-N-N," just managing to add the "Y" as the clock hit nine seconds.

The door leading back to the reception area opened, the lights flickering on above us as a resounding triumph of trumpets rang out overhead.

"We did it!" I cried. I swirled on my heel. Now to get the vampires out of here...

Only I'd taken just a step back inside before a red laser light positioned above the center cell door pointed straight at me—and sliced through my arm.

Chapter Twenty-Two

*I*n Sheriff Roan's station, Roan and Abdel were shouting at one another, arguing about whether or not Abdel should have called in the county for backup when Arjun had reported the locked escape room building door—he hadn't—and how they were going to report Fred's death and Karter's accident.

Then there was the matter of Karter's involvement in the death of Ginny Kincaid.

It was well past midnight at this point, but Roan had just gotten back from the scene, Doc Day and he escorting Karter to the single jail cell, where the out-of-towner still sat as this argument took place.

I looked at my left arm. There was a bit of pink flesh I'd had to heal as soon as I'd been able from a gash the actual live laser weapon had dug into my skin, but most of it had bounced off the rather large stone scale nearing my elbow, sending the laser beam flying up into the ceiling and burning a whole right through the tiles.

That had not been a part of the original escape room design. Some harmless laser lights, maybe, but not the kind that actually caused any damage—unless you stared straight at them for a while, I supposed.

Cable had acted fast. He'd offered me an arm, carrying Broomie in his other hand, and dragged me outside. We'd shouted at the growing crowd that they needed help inside, but Cable continued to guide me down the block, encouraging me to try my magic whenever I could.

I'd rotated between using my right hand to put pressure on the wound on my left arm and shaking it out to try my simple "WOLG" spell until finally, two blocks down, my magic returned and I healed the wound.

Broomie had cooed then, stretching her every fiber as if waking from a long nap.

Nuzzling my cheek to bristles, I'd been surprised to find that she nuzzled not only me back, but Cable as well.

His face had alit with amusement instead of fear for once.

"Thank goodness," he'd told me.

"I'll say." I'd turned around and waved at my friends as they'd made their way closer, away from the source of our torment. Draven had leaned on Faine and Qarinah on Roan, Arjun, Abdel, Chione, and Zashil dragging Karter's limp form to the middle of the street. "Over here!" I'd shouted.

They'd all made their way to me without question, Doc Day sliding in beside the unconscious Karter and doing a preliminary on him as he was carried along.

"He's breathing," she'd said to me.

I'd nodded. "LAEH!" With my shaking arms, my enchantment had flown out to the man, and though it had taken a little effort—which indicated how close he'd been to dying—after a minute, his eyes had popped open and he'd shot up, coughing, writhing and having to be soothed and put back down on his feet.

Draven's and Qarinah's steps had grown surer as they'd neared, their hair darker, their skin smoother and paler. They hadn't needed my help. They'd just needed to be away from that stuff.

I'd smiled at them, and Draven had blinked fiercely as if taken aback, biting the corner of his lip with the sharp fang he'd started to lose inside the building.

Then my smile had fallen. "Ginny?"

Everyone had turned to look over their shoulders. "We don't know," Roan had said. "After the laser went off, we couldn't see her anymore."

"Might have scared her so much, she couldn't fight to keep visible anymore," Cable had offered.

"Or she fled," Draven had snapped, crossing his arms over his chest.

Either had seemed a real possibility at this point.

Now that I knew my friends were safe, it was just a matter of confirming a few more things before I could get some sleep.

"Well, you could either have a few more people find out about us, or you can have a few dead citizens on your hands," said Roan over his shoulder as he shuffled over to me.

Abdel seemed tired, which was strange for a mummy who could live forever if his wrappings remained intact. "You could have made the call, but you deferred to me."

Chione cajoled her grandfather in quiet tones, directing him toward the door. She nodded at me and Doc Day.

Abdel scowled at Roan but nodded curtly at me. "Dahlia," he said. "Thanks for solving this case again. Maybe I should make *you* sheriff."

I laughed, but he didn't seem to be kidding.

"No, thank you," I said. "I have enough on my plate."

"Well, Luna Lane owes you its thanks." Abdel straightened his suitcoat and then left, Chione on his heels.

"You should get home," said Doc Day. "It's been a long day."

"You're not taking Karter to the Creekdale hospital?" I asked.

"And have even more questions pointed this way right now? I'll leave the politics to the civil servants."

She waved a hand in the air and packed up her medical bag. "He seems fine. I might not even care if a man who helped kill our dear Virginia isn't fine regardless."

Roan shot her a look, but she shrugged and bid us goodnight.

The station went quiet.

Roan let out a sigh and sat down, sending his office chair rolling backward. "Well, this is a pickle."

"To put it mildly." I stood and pointed to the single jail cell. "Do you mind if I ask him a few questions?"

"By all means." Roan gestured for me to go ahead. "Sherriff Poplar," he added. But a wicked grin was on his lips.

I stuck my tongue out at him and moved around the desk, dragging my chair with me to sit it in front of the holding cell.

Beside Karter—even more disheveled if that were possible—on the jail cell cot was Broomie, curled up in a circle and snoring loudly. She'd been there before Karter had been dumped inside and I hadn't had the heart to move her.

Karter sat at the other end of the cot, staring at her. I almost thought he hadn't noticed my approach.

"So… Witches are real?" he said.

"We are." I patted my head. "Though I'm still missing my hat." I grimaced. No one had found it in the escape room after a thorough search done by

275

normies—Cable and Todd and a few others were still trying to clean the place more thoroughly of the para-paranormal, power-blasting the porous surfaces.

He looked up at me, the exhaustion dulling his eyes. "You were how Fred got that place up and running so fast?"

"Yup." My jaw tensed. "I cast an enchantment that brought to life the designs on his phone…"

"The ones that were never supposed to be actually constructed." Karter let out a deep breath. So I'd been right about that. "I thought the construction team would notice and alert him—even if he used a shoddy operation, surely, they wouldn't be investing in crushing granite and actual laser parts. Then he might see her birthday, her name…"

I wondered if my enchantment had done the work to craft those out of bits of the bowling alley, like Cable's hair turned into a hat and his flesh into gloves. I doubted they had been among the materials delivered, especially if Fred was used to supplying for the safer, usual design.

"You couldn't have foreseen I'd bring the designs to life without knowing about the harm they could do—"

"It doesn't matter. I got my just desserts with that. Fred got his." Karter rubbed at his neck, though there were no bruises anymore.

"You knew Ginny's birthday?" I asked.

"I barely knew her at all. I actually was introduced to his other fiancée—his now ex-wife. I think Ginny really was a side piece. Or maybe Fred wanted to see whose parents had more money, decide which to actually marry in the end, I don't know." He gripped the edge of the cot tightly. "But I couldn't let it go. I followed the case obsessively—I got her birthdate from that. No one figured it was anything but an accident. The shed collapsed and then caught on fire. Struck by lightning or maybe the broken lantern. They actually believed Fred when he said that he barely knew her. She hadn't introduced him to her parents—a deliberate choice on Fred's part—so they couldn't even verify the relationship had been genuine. The police didn't know he'd had the shed built and designed—never pegged me as the designer. None of the shady workmen spoke up. We got away with it."

"An autopsy didn't reveal she was strangled?" I asked.

"There was the mangled leg, the blow to her head—the body was too burnt up to really reveal anything. The damage to the neck vertebrae was figured to have happened in the fall from the loft." He really *had* studied up on this case. "It didn't... It didn't even bother Fred. In all my years with him, I'd known him to be a charming man, hiding a scheming personality—but murder?" He sighed. "It wasn't like he took to it or kept at it, as far as I knew, but he wasn't plagued by guilt."

"Like you were?"

He nodded.

"Not enough to turn yourself in, though."

Karter fiddled with his hands on his lap. "I thought about it. Nearly every day—but I never did it."

"You kept working with Fred?"

"I had no choice!" He looked up at me now, desperate. "Fred threatened to pin it all on me if I spoke up, if I walked away. He wanted me where he could keep an eye on me, but he also just wanted to take advantage of me. He ruined my life. I couldn't bring myself to date anyone, couldn't have any friends. It was all Fred and his problems and the murder in my head all the time."

"You helped him take Ginny's life entirely." I stopped him before he could defend himself. "You didn't stop him. And supposing you couldn't do that —you still didn't turn him in. You *helped* him because you were scared."

Karter had nothing more to say to that.

Broomie stretched then, my voice having grown louder and stirring her from her sleep. She saw me and perked up, flying out from between the bars with ease and into my hands.

"Thanks for saving my life," said Karter. "They explained…" He left the rest unsaid.

"May you spend the rest of it trying to make up for what you did," I added.

Karter's sobbing echoed out behind me as I offered Roan a slight wave and went on my way.

Broomie glided us smoothly homeward above the sidewalks of Luna Lane, the night mostly over at this point.

When I got there, my heart clenched somewhat at the sight of a wicked face glowing out at me from the dark on my front step.

Someone had carved my atrocious pumpkin and turned him into a Jack-o-Lantern. He seemed to relish the spine-tingling expression on his face.

"Hello?" I called out, landing on my feet and pushing open the front door. Broomie floated behind me cautiously.

Inside, in the middle of the floor on my rune circle, was my witch's hat.

I picked it up, inspected it for anything wrong with it, and slid it on my head. On the ground beneath where the hat had been was a pile of purple and silver fabric. I picked it up. It was a dress.

"I asked Spindra to make it."

Ginny's voice echoed out from the darkness. I spun around, clutching the dress to my chest.

She sat there—dressed like someone from the late twentieth century, not the beginning of it, atop my table full of potions and flasks. Since she wasn't corporeal at the moment, she didn't so much as jostle a single one of them.

"I don't... I don't understand," I said.

"For Halloween." Ginny shrugged and jumped down to her feet, only her ghostly soles didn't touch the floor at all. "I'd thought maybe I could celebrate it with you this year—before Fred rolled into town, anyway."

She spun around and her casual clothes turned into something more at home at a modern prom, a pale yellow, sleeveless dress that matched her hair. "I can change clothes like this—and I suppose you could wave those arms of yours and spin an enchantment to do the same. But I wanted to get something for you." She tucked her long hair behind her ear. "A gift. For a friend."

"Spindra took your commission after…?"

"Well, she'd already finished making it by the time I swung by. Some gut feeling you'd need it this year. I explained ordering a dress for you had been my original aim when I'd initially stopped by and found her and Fred… Well, I told her the full story and I apologized." She chuckled, though it didn't quite reach her eyes. "She told me, 'Darling, good riddance, then. No enemy of woman should walk away from murder. I only regret not making him a snack.'"

My heart clenching, I clutched the dress to my chest. It was lovely. And I *had* been neglecting to make Halloween much of a special occasion since my mom had died.

"Do you think Zashil and Javier will move away again?" she asked.

I thought about poor Zashil after the ordeal, Javier comforting him as I'd worked on Karter. "Probably," I said. "But he used to be so eager to get out of here and see the whole wide world. I don't know why he'd ever thought to squander that freedom. He and Javier will be okay."

I didn't know how I knew that, but it was true.

"I didn't mean to ruin his dream," Ginny said. "I was so lost in my own hatred—"

"We understand," I said. "I do—I know Zashil will, too. You saved him from getting in deep with a criminal, too. He'll be sure to appreciate that. If not now, then someday."

"Sure," she said, tucking her hands behind her back and shuffling her feet.

"Ginny, I—"

"I know. You can't forgive me. I can't go to jail, but I shouldn't be forgiven, either."

"That's not what I was going to say." I stared down at the dress and said, "EGNAHC," indicating for it and my solid black dress to swap. They did, my hair curling into ringlets as I spun around, my mere vision of what I'd wanted enough to make it all happen.

Maybe I really was growing stronger with practice.

Broomie cooed appreciatively, and Ginny clapped her hands silently. "Lovely!" she said.

"Thank you," I told her, tossing my other dress

atop the nearby table. "It's beautiful. Did you carve the Jack-o-Lantern, too?"

She grinned. "You noticed?"

"Halloween isn't until tomorrow." Mom's cuckoo clock struck and reminded me it was seven in the morning. "Well, I mean, I don't celebrate until later today."

"I might not have another day," she said softly. "My reason for staying behind—it's been accomplished. Now, whatever punishment awaits me on the other side…"

"But Karter?" I offered.

"I heard what he said to you," she said. "After I set this up, I was going to go get you, but I saw where you were and well… I hid and listened. He'll get his punishment. Seems like he punished himself more than Fred anyway." She twirled a bit of gauzy yellow fabric around her finger.

"I'm so used to seeing you all in white," I said. "But yellow looks good on you too."

"Thanks." She fingered a necklace at her clavicle and I realized it was the same red jewel from the brooch she'd worn all those years. She saw me looking at it. It was so familiar. "A gift," she said. "From your mother."

"*My* mother?" I asked.

"She knew what I was," she said softly. "She said this would keep the earth from weighing too heavily on me, whatever that meant. I liked it, so I wore it, fashioned it into my brooch. But I felt… I guess I felt a little less urgency after that. I felt more at peace, more at home in Luna Lane."

The earth weighing on her? Like a bolt of lightning, I realized. The Poplar crest in the potions book, the motto: *Sit tibi terra levis.* What had Cable told me that meant? *"May the earth rest lightly on you."* A blessing for a funeral.

"I'm glad," I said, feeling suddenly as if that motto weren't so foreboding after all. For Virginia, it was a blessing, the earth—and the crime that had put her beneath it—not weighing her down. "That you feel at peace here."

"Do you think I could stay?" she asked, already wincing at what she thought would be my answer.

"I don't know," I said. "I know if you left, I'd miss my friend. Have any other regrets?" I asked, maybe a little too hopefully.

"Putting you all in harms' way," she said simply.

I extended a hand out toward her and she took it in hers, her icy cold hand becoming corporeal. I twirled her, as if spinning her to ballroom music that only I could hear. "Then stay. At least for one more day. Someone has to celebrate Halloween with me later tonight."

Giggling, she took a turn at spinning me, my own laughter bubbling out into the muted glow of this Halloween twilight.

Join the Spooky Games Club in Potions and Playing Cards!

Fixated on researching ways to break her curse once and for all, jinxed witch and do-gooder Dahlia Poplar doesn't know how well she'll do in the upcoming Euchre Tournament, the Luna Lane

Spooky Games Club's first sponsored event. With visiting professor Cable Woodward due to depart to spend more of his sabbatical on the road, Dahlia can't admit that he may be the reason she's so determined to finally leave behind the cozy comforts of home.

Unfortunately, her efforts stir up unwanted attention from the one who cursed Dahlia to begin with, the evil witch whose shadow has loomed over all of the dreadful events in Luna Lane. When the tournament ends prematurely, there's a body charred to ashes, and Dahlia takes it upon herself to figure out if the wicked witch is behind the disaster. Somehow, she needs to brew the right potion to break her curse while solving the paranormal message encoded in the club's playing cards, all while keeping her loved ones safe.

Her very life may be the ante she risks to get to the bottom of everything that's been plaguing her since birth—and if she can't bluff her way to winning, Dahlia Poplar may prove to be the dead card that's no longer in play.

About the Author

Amy McNulty is an editor and author of books that run the gamut from YA speculative fiction to contemporary romance. A lifelong fiction fanatic, she fangirls over books, anime, manga, comics, movies, games, and TV shows from her home state of Wisconsin. When not reviewing anime professionally or editing her clients' novels, she's busy fulfilling her dream by crafting fantastical worlds of her own.

Sign up for Amy's newsletter to receive news and exclusive information about her current and upcoming projects. Get a free YA romantic sci-fi novelette when you do!

Find her at amymcnulty.com and follow her on social media:

amazon.com/author/amymcnulty

bookbub.com/authors/amy-mcnulty

facebook.com/AmyMcNultyAuthor

twitter.com/mcnultyamy

instagram.com/mcnulty.amy

pinterest.com/authoramymc

Look for More Mystery Fiction Reads
from Crimson Fox Publishing

Crimson Fox
PUBLISHING

Old Flames

ELISA KEYSTON

Lose yourself in the magical forests and charming towns of the Pacific Northwest, where picturesque Victorian homes hide mysteries spanning decades, faeries watch

from the trees, and romance awaits... for those bold enough to seek it.

Laney isn't looking for love. She's perfectly happy with the life she's built for herself in the little town of Foreston, Washington. She's a successful businesswoman, the owner of an alterations shop with a clientele across the northwest. She's the chair of the local Victorian house museum's annual fashion show. And she has a reputation for a magic touch: the rumor around town is that anyone who wears one of the period costumes she designs in her spare time will be blessed with good luck.

That's what they say, anyway. Laney knows the truth is a bit more complicated—anything she wills while sewing has a tendency of coming to pass. It's a supernatural gift from the fae who are said to inhabit the woods surrounding the Paine Estate, and it's taught her to keep a guard on her notorious redheaded temper. But keeping her temper becomes difficult when journalist Paul Nelson comes to town to do a feature about the museum. With his stunning good looks and swoon-worthy English accent, Paul is charming, irresistible... and just so happens to be Laney's ex.

Laney wants nothing more than to keep Paul at arm's length, but when she stumbles across a series of break-ins at the museum, she may have no choice but to trust the dashing reporter who once broke her heart to help her catch the culprit. And when a nearby forest fire threatens the safety of the town—and of the woods—will Laney be able to put her old feelings aside in order to protect the magic of Foreston? Or will that same magic lead to an unexpected happy ending?

With its unique blend of small-town romance, cozy mystery, and light fantasy, the Northwest Magic series is sure to delight anyone who believes in faery gifts and happily-ever-afters. Read FREE in Kindle Unlimited and get lost in the magic now!

The Vainest Knife

K.L. TEAL

After the tragic suicide of Mina's old friend Ryder, she reunites with the rest of her high school friends, John and Mario, to spend five days at John's secluded cabin in the woods to process their loss. Though she had spent time at the cabin with her friends years ago, something about the place now causes Mina to feel uneasy. Strange, unexplained events start to occur that Mina's friends are quick to brush off. But the more Mina delves into the history of the house, her relationships with her friends, and her own psyche, more unsettling details begin to unravel.

When one of her friends disappears under mysterious circumstances, Mina starts to become paranoid. She believes the house is haunted, but her friends seem to think there is something much more sinister at work caused by a living person. As the friends search for answers, Mina becomes increasingly targeted by the supernatural forces of the house. Her desperation to find the truth could be what ultimately saves her—or it could spiral her into complete and utter insanity.

The Never Veil Series:

Nobody's Goddess

Nobody's Lady

Nobody's Pawn

The Blood, Bloom, & Water Series:

Fangs & Fins

Salt & Venom

Iron & Aqua

Tears & Cruor

The Fall Far from the Tree Duology:

Fall Far from the Tree

Turn to Dust and Ashes

Ballad of the Beanstalk

Josie's Coat

Made in the USA
Middletown, DE
30 June 2021

43365027R00179